"What would I do without you, Luke Rivers?"

"You won't ever need to find that out, Kate Logan." Luke's arms encircled her waist and he kissed the tip of her nose. His smile was tender. "There must have been something in the air last night. First us, and now your father and Mrs. Murphy."

"About us . . ." Kate began carefully. "Luke, I value your friendship. You've helped me so much." She drew in a steadying breath, and her eyes avoided his. "But I hope you realize that when I asked you to marry me, I . . . I didn't actually mean it."

He went very still and for the longest moment of Kate's life, he said nothing. "I took you seriously, Kate."

She forced a light laugh. "I'm not going to hold you to your promise, Luke."

He shook his head, stroking the side of his jaw. "My word is my word and I stand firm on it."

Debbie Macomber is an American writer born in the state of Washington, where she still lives. She and her electrician husband have four children, all of them teenagers. They also support a menagerie that includes horses, cats, a dog and some guinea pigs. Debbie's successful writing career actually started in childhood, when her brother copied—and sold—her diary! She's gone on to a considerably wider readership since then, as a prolific and popular author published in several different romance lines. She says she wrote her first book because she fell in love with Harlequin Romances—and wanted to write her own.

Country Bride is the sequel to *A Little Bit Country* (Harlequin Romance 3038).

Books by Debbie Macomber

HARLEQUIN ROMANCE
2768—THE MATCHMAKERS
2835—LOVE BY DEGREE
2993—YOURS AND MINE
3038—A LITTLE BIT COUNTRY

Don't miss any of our special offers. Write to us at the following address for information on our newest releases.

Harlequin Reader Service
901 Fuhrmann Blvd., P.O. Box 1397, Buffalo, NY 14240
Canadian address: P.O. Box 603,
Fort Erie, Ont. L2A 5X3

Country
Bride

Debbie Macomber

Harlequin Books

TORONTO • NEW YORK • LONDON
AMSTERDAM • PARIS • SYDNEY • HAMBURG
STOCKHOLM • ATHENS • TOKYO • MILAN

ISBN 0-373-03059-2

Harlequin Romance first edition June 1990

CHAPTER ONE

"I NOW PRONOUNCE YOU husband and wife."

A burst of organ music crescendoed through the largest church in Nightingale, Oregon, as a murmur of shared happiness rose from the excited congregation.

Standing at the altar, Clay Franklin claimed his right to kiss Rorie Campbell Franklin, his bride.

Kate Logan did her best to look delighted for her friends, even though she felt as if a giant fist had been slammed into her stomach. Tears gathered in her eyes and she lowered her gaze, unable to watch as the man she'd loved most of her life wrapped his arm around his new bride's waist.

Clay should be marrying me, Kate cried silently. *I should be the one he's looking at so tenderly. Me!* During the past few weeks, Kate had repeatedly reassured herself that she'd done the right thing in stepping aside to bring Clay and Rorie together. But that fact didn't lessen her pain now. Kate loved Clay, and that wasn't ever going to change. He was her best friend and confidant, her compass, her North Star. And now Clay was married to another woman— someone he loved far more than he could ever care for Kate.

A clean white handkerchief was thrust into her hand by Luke Rivers, her father's foreman. Kate knew he'd been waiting for this moment, convinced she'd dissolve into a puddle of tears.

She declined the use of his kerchief by gently shaking her head.

"I'm here," he whispered in her ear.

"So is half of Nightingale," she returned wryly. Luke seemed determined to rescue her from this pain—as if that was possible. All she wanted was to survive this day with her dignity intact, and his open sympathy threatened the outward composure she'd painfully mustered.

"You're doing fine."

"Luke," she muttered, "stop making a fuss over me. Please." She'd managed to get through the ceremony without breaking down. The last thing she needed now was to have Luke calling attention to her.

The ironic thing was that Kate had been the one responsible for bringing Clay and Rorie together. She should be feeling noble and jubilant and honorable. But the only emotion she felt was a deep, abiding sense of loss.

Rorie and Clay walked down the center aisle, and from somewhere deep inside her, Kate found the strength to raise her head and smile blindly in their direction. Luke's hands gripped her shoulders as though to lend her strength. His concern should have been a comfort, but it wasn't.

"I'll walk you to the reception hall," Luke said, slipping his arm through hers.

"I'm perfectly capable of making it there on my own," she snapped, not wanting his pity. She would have argued more, but since they were sitting near the front of the church, they were among the first to be ushered out. Holding her head high, Kate walked past her friends and neighbors, doing her best to appear cheerful and serene.

At least she *looked* her best; Kate had made certain of that. She'd curled her thick blond hair until it lightly brushed her shoulders. The style emphasized her blue eyes and sculptured cheekbones. She'd shopped long and hard for the perfect dress for this wedding and had found one that enhanced her tiny waist and outlined her trim figure. The minute she'd tried on the soft blue silk and viewed herself in the mirror, Kate had known the dress was perfect. Although the lines were simple, the look was both classic and sophisticated, a look she'd never bothered to cultivate before. Too often in the past, she'd been mistaken for a teenager mostly, she supposed, because she dressed the part. Now, she was a woman though, and she had the broken heart to prove it.

Kate paused in the church vestibule, waiting for her father. Devin was sitting with Dorothea Murphy, his widow friend. Her father's interest in the older woman was something of a mystery to Kate. Tall and plump and outspoken, she was completely unlike Kate's late mother, who'd been delicate and reserved. Kate sometimes wondered what it was about Dorothea that so strongly attracted her father. The two had been seeing a lot of each other in recent weeks, but the possibility of their contemplating marriage filled Kate with a sudden, overwhelming sense of alarm. Kate pushed the thought from her mind. Losing Clay was all she could deal with right now.

"Are you all right, Princess?" Devin asked when he joined her.

"I wish everyone would stop worrying about me. I'm fine." It wasn't the truth, but Kate was well aware that she had to put on a breezy, unconcerned front. At least for the next few hours.

Her father patted her hand gently. "I know how hard this is for you. Do you want to go to the reception or would you prefer to head home?" His eyes were warm and sympathetic, and Kate felt a rush of love for him. A part of her longed to slip away unnoticed, but she couldn't and she knew it.

"Kate's already agreed to accompany me," Luke inserted, daring her to contradict him.

Indignation rose inside her. Instead of helping, Luke was making everything worse. The pain of watching Clay pledge his life to another woman was difficult enough, without Luke's unsought demands.

"I'm pleased to hear that," Devin Logan said, looking relieved. He smiled as he slipped his arm around Dorothea's thick waist. "Mrs. Murphy invited me to sit with her and, frankly, I was looking forward to doing so." He released Kate's hand, kissed her on the cheek, then strolled nonchalantly away.

"Shall we?" Grinning, Luke reached for Kate's limp hand and tucked it into the crook of his arm. As if they'd been a couple for years, he casually led the way out of the church.

The early evening air was crisp and clear. Autumn had crested on an October tide of bronze and gold leaves, huge pumpkins and early twilights. Normally, this time of year invigorated Kate. If she hadn't been fortifying herself against Clay's wedding, she could have appreciated the season more.

The walk across the parking lot to the reception hall was a short one. Kate didn't say another word to Luke, mentally preparing herself for the coming encounter with Clay and his bride. With each step her heart grew heavier. Rorie had asked her to be a bridesmaid, and although Kate was honored by the request, she'd declined. Rorie understood and hadn't pressured her. Despite the fact that they both loved the same man, Rorie and Kate had become close. Their friendship made everything more difficult for Kate, yet somehow easier, too.

By the time they reached the old brick building, Kate's pulse was so loud it echoed like a drum in her ear. Just outside the double doors leading into the hall, she stopped abruptly.

"I can't go in there," she told Luke. Panic had worked its way into her voice, which was low and trembling. "I can't face them and pretend... I just can't do it."

"You can—I'll help you."

"How can you possibly know what I can and can't do?" she demanded, wanting to bury her face in her hands and weep. These past few hours had taken their toll and she couldn't keep up the charade much longer. Luke gazed down on her and for the briefest of moments, his eyes registered sympathy and regret.

"You can go in there and you will," he repeated.

Kate saw determination in his serious dark eyes and swallowed an angry retort, knowing he was right.

At six feet, Luke towered over her, and the hard set of his mouth did more than hint at determination and a will of iron. "If you don't attend the reception, everyone in Nightingale will talk. Is that what you want?"

"Yes," she cried, then lowered her head, battling down wave after wave of depression and self-pity that threatened to swamp her. "No," she said reluctantly, loath to agree with him.

"I'm here for you, Kate. Lean on me for once in your life, and let me help you through the next few hours."

"I'm doing fine. I—"

He wouldn't allow her to finish. "Quit fighting me. I'm your friend, remember?"

His words, hushed and tender, brought a burning to her eyes. Her fingers tightened around his arm and she nodded, calling upon a reserve of strength she didn't know she possessed. "Just don't be so bossy with me. Please. I can bear almost anything but that." She'd made it through the wedding ceremony on her own reserves of strength. Now she needed someone at her side to help her appear strong and steady when she felt as though the entire universe was pitching and heaving.

"Anything you say, Princess."

Although she'd objected earlier, she felt comforted by his strong arm pressing against her. She heard his voice, as if from a distance, too preoccupied with her own pain to respond to his gentle concern. But his presence restored her determination to acquit herself well during the long evening ahead.

"Only Daddy calls me Princess," she said distract-edly.

"You mind?"

"I don't know... I suppose it's all right."

"Good." His fingers intertwined with hers as he led her into the brightly decorated reception hall.

The next half hour was a blur. Drawing upon Luke's silent strength, Kate managed to make it through the reception line without a problem. Still, her knees felt shaky by the time she reached Clay, who kissed her cheek and thanked her for being so wonderful. Kate certainly didn't *feel* wonderful—even particularly admirable—but she smiled. And she was sincere when she offered Clay and Rorie her very best wishes.

Somehow Luke must have known how frail she felt because he took her hand and led her to one of the round lace-covered tables. His fingers were cool and callused, while Kate's were damp with her stubborn determination to hide her pain.

Wordlessly, she sat beside Luke until the cake had been cut and the first piece ceremonially fed to the bride and groom. The scene before her flickered like an old silent movie. Kate held herself still, trying not to feel anything, but not succeeding.

"Would you like me to get you something to eat?" Luke asked, when a line formed to gather refreshments.

She stared at him, hardly able to comprehend his words. Then she blinked and her eyes traveled across the hall to the three-tiered heart-shaped wedding cake. "No," she said automatically.

"When was the last time you ate?"

Kate didn't remember. She shrugged. "Breakfast, I guess." As she spoke she realized that wasn't true. Dinner the night before was the last time she'd eaten. No wonder she felt so shaky and light-headed.

"I'm getting you some wedding cake," Luke announced grimly.

"Don't. I'm—I'm not hungry."

He was doing it again! Taking over, making decisions on her behalf because he felt sorry for her. She would have argued with him, but he was already walking away, blithely unaware of her frustration.

Kate watched him, suddenly seeing him with fresh eyes. Luke Rivers had lived and worked on the Circle

L for a decade, but Kate knew next to nothing of his past. His official title was foreman, but he was much more than that. He'd initiated several successful cattle-breeding programs and had been involved in a profit-sharing venture with her father almost from the first. Devin had often remarked that Luke was more than capable of maintaining his own spread. But year after year, he continued to stay at the Circle L. This realization—that she knew so little of his past and even less about his thoughts and plans—shocked Kate. He'd always been just plain Luke. And he'd always been around, or so it seemed. She considered him a good friend, yet she hardly knew him. Not really. Especially considering the length of time he'd been at the Circle L.

She had to admit that Luke puzzled her. He was handsome enough, but he rarely dated any woman for long, although plenty of Nightingale's finest had made their interest obvious. He was a "catch" who refused to play ball. He could be as tough as leather and mean as a saddle sore when the mood struck him, but it seldom did. Tall, lean and rugged adequately described him on the surface. It was what lay below that piqued her interest now.

Kate's musings about Luke were disrupted by the man himself as he pulled out the chair beside her and sat down. He pushed a delicate china plate filled with cheese and mixed nuts in her direction.

"I thought you were bringing me cake." His own plate was loaded with a huge piece, in addition to a few nuts and pastel mints.

"I brought you some protein instead. Sugar's the last thing you need on an empty stomach."

"I don't believe you," she muttered, her sarcasm fueled by his arrogance. "First you insist on bringing me cake, and then just when I'm looking forward to sampling it, you decide I shouldn't be eating sweets."

Luke ignored her, slicing into a thick piece of cake with the side of his fork. "Just a minute ago, you claimed it would be a waste of time for me to bring you anything. Fact is, you downright refused to eat."

"That . . . was before."

He smiled, and that knowing cocky smile of his infuriated her.

"You'll feel sick if you eat sugar," he announced in an authoritative voice.

So much for helping her through this evening! All he seemed to want to do was quarrel. "Apparently you know how my stomach is going to react to certain food groups. You amaze me, Luke Rivers. You honestly amaze me. I had no idea you knew so much about my body's metabolism."

"You'd be shocked if I told you all the things I know about you and your body, Princess."

Kate stood abruptly. "I don't think it's a good idea for you to call me that. I'm not your 'Princess.' I'm a woman, not a little girl."

"Honey, you don't need to tell me that. I already know. Now sit down." His tone was brusque, and his smile humorless.

"I'll stand if I choose."

"Fine then. Look like a fool, if that's what you want."

No sooner had the words left his lips than she limply lowered herself back into the chair. The fight had gone out of her as quickly as it had come. Absently she scooped up a handful of nuts and chewed them vigorously, taking her frustration out on them.

Luke pushed his plate aside and reached for her hand, squeezing it gently. ''I'm your friend. I've always been your friend and I'll continue to be your friend as long as I live. Don't ever doubt that.''

Kate's eyes misted and her throat tightened painfully. ''I know. It's just that this is so much more . . . exhausting than I thought it would be.''

Voices drew Kate's eyes to the front of the room, where Clay and Rorie were toasting each other with tall, thin glasses of sparkling champagne. Soon flutes were being delivered around the room. Kate took one, holding the long stem with both hands as if the champagne would lend her strength.

When the newlyweds were toasted, she took a sip. It bubbled and fizzed inside her mouth, then slid easily down her throat.

The soft strains of a violin drifted around the hall, and mesmerized, Kate watched as Clay claimed his bride and led her onto the dance floor. Just watching the couple, so much in love, with eyes only for each other, heaped an extra burden of pain on Kate's thin shoulders. She looked away and, when she did, her gaze met Luke's. She tried to smile, to convince him she wasn't feeling a thing, but the effort was a poor one. Ready tears brimmed at the corners of her eyes and she lowered her head, not wanting anyone to notice them, least of all Luke. He'd been wonderful; he'd been terrible. Kate couldn't decide which.

Soon others joined Clay and Rorie. First the matron of honor and then the bridesmaids and groomsmen, each couple swirling around the polished floor with practiced ease.

Luke got to his feet, walked to Kate's side, and offered her his hand. His eyes held hers, silently demanding that she dance with him. Kate longed to tell him no, but she didn't have the energy to argue. It was simpler to comply than try to explain why she couldn't.

Together they approached the outskirts of the dance floor and Luke skillfully turned her into his arms.

''Everything's going to be all right,'' he whispered as his hand slipped around her waist.

Kate managed a nod, grateful for his concern. She needed Luke this evening more than she'd realized. One thing was certain—she'd never make it through the remainder of the night without him.

During the past several years, Luke had danced with Kate any number of times. She'd never given it a second thought. Now they danced one number and then another, but when she slipped into his embrace a third time, and his fingers spread across the small of her back, a shiver of unexpected awareness skidded up her spine. Kate paused, confused. Her steps faltered and in what seemed like an effort to help her, Luke pulled her closer. Soon their bodies were so close together Kate could hear the steady beat of Luke's heart against her own. The quickening rate of his pulse told her he was experiencing the same rush of excitement she was.

Kate felt so light-headed she was almost giddy. Luke's arms were warm and secure, a solid foundation to hold on to when her world had been abruptly kicked off its axis. It might have been selfish, but Kate needed that warmth, that security. Smiling up at him, she closed her eyes and surrendered to the warm sensations carried on the soft, lilting music.

"Kate, there's something I need to tell you about the Circle L—"

She pressed her fingers against his lips, afraid that words would ruin this feeling. Arms twined around his neck, she grazed his jaw with the side of her face, reveling in the feel of him. Male and strong. Lean and hard.

"All right," he whispered, "we'll talk about it later."

They continued dancing and Luke rubbed his face against her hair, mussing it slightly, but Kate didn't mind.

Like a contented cat, she purred softly, the low sound coming from deep in her throat. The music ended all too quickly and with heavy reluctance, she dropped her arms and backed up one small step. Silently they stood more than an inch apart until the music resumed, giving them the necessary excuse to reach for each other once again.

But this time Kate made an effort to work out what was happening between them. Knowing how much she loved Clay, Luke was determined to help her through the evening. Yes, that had to be it. And doing a fine job, too. She felt ... marvelous. It didn't make sense to her that she should experience this strong, unexpectedly sensual attraction to Luke, but at the moment she didn't care. He was concerned and gentle and she needed him.

They remained as they were, not speaking, savoring these warm sensations, until Kate lost count of the number of dances they'd shared.

When the band took a ten-minute break, Luke released her with an unwillingness that made her heart soar. As though he couldn't bear to be separated from her, he reached for her hand, lacing her soft fingers with his strong ones.

He was leading her back to their table when they were interrupted by Betty Hammond, a pert blonde, who'd hurried toward them. "Hello, Luke," she said, ignoring Kate.

"Betty." He dipped his head politely, but it was clear he didn't appreciate the intrusion.

The other woman placed a proprietary hand on his arm. "You promised me a dance, remember?"

Kate's eyes swiveled from Betty, who was pouting prettily, to Luke who looked testy and impatient.

"If you'll excuse me a minute, I'm going to get something to drink," Kate said. Her throat was parched and she didn't want to be left standing alone when the music started and Betty walked off with Luke.

The fruit punch was cold and refreshing, but she still felt warm. Kate decided to walk outside and let the cool night air clear her mind. She didn't really understand what was happening between her and Luke, but she thought it probably had to do with the confused state of her emotions.

The stars glittered like frost diamonds against a velvety black sky. Kate stood in the crisp evening air with her arms wrapped around her waist, gazing up at the heavens. She didn't hear Luke until he stepped behind her and lightly rested his hands on her shoulders. "I couldn't find you," he said in a voice that was softly accusing.

Kate didn't want to discuss Betty Hammond. For as long as she could remember, the other woman had been going out of her way to attract him.

"It's beautiful out tonight, isn't it?" she asked instead. Instinctively she nestled closer to Luke, reclining against the lean strength of his body, seeking his warmth.

"Beautiful," he repeated, running his hands down the length of her arms.

How content she felt with Luke, how comfortable—the way she imagined people felt when they'd been married twenty years. But along with this familiar sense of ease, she experienced a prickle of anticipation. Her feelings contradicted themselves, she realized wryly. Secure and steady, and at the same time this growing sense of giddy excitement. It must be that glass of champagne, she decided.

The band started playing again and the sweet sounds of the music wafted outside. Gently Luke turned her to face him, slipping his hands around her as if to dance. Her arms reached for his neck, resuming their earlier position.

"We should talk," he whispered close to her ear.

"No," she murmured with a sigh. Finding her way back into Luke's arms was like arriving home after an extended vacation. It seemed the most natural thing in the world to stand on the tips of her toes and brush her moist lips over his. Then she realized what she'd done. Her eyes rounded and she abruptly stepped back, her heart hammering inside her chest.

Neither spoke. In the light that spilled from the hall windows, they stared at each other, searching. Kate didn't know what her eyes told Luke, but his own were clouded with uncertainty. Kate half expected him to chastise her, or to tease her for behaving like such a flirt. Instead he reached for her once more, his eyes challenging her to stop him.

She couldn't.

The warmth of his mouth on hers produced a small sigh of welcome as her eyes slid languidly shut; she felt transported into a dreamworld, one she had never visited before. This couldn't actually be happening, she told herself, and yet it felt so very real. And so right.

Luke's kiss was surprisingly tender, unlike anything she'd expected. He held her as though she were made of the most delicate bone china and might shatter at the slightest pressure.

"My darling Kate," he breathed against her hair, "I've dreamed of this so often."

"You have?" To her own ears, her voice sounded as though it came from far, far away. Her head was swimming. If this was a dream, then she didn't want it to end. Sighing, she smiled beguilingly up at him.

"You little tease," he said, and laughed softly. He rained light kisses on her forehead, the corners of her eyes and her cheek, until she interrupted his meandering lips, seeking his mouth with her own.

He seemed to want the kiss as much as she did. But apparently saw no need to rush the experience, as if he feared hurrying would spoil it. Kate's mouth parted softly, inviting a deeper union. His willing compliance was so effective it buckled her knees.

"Kate?" Still holding her, he drew back, tilting his head to study her. Boldly she met his look, her eyes dancing with mischief. If he'd been kissing her out of pity, she was past caring.

A long moment passed before a slow, thoughtful smile played across his lips. "I think I'd better get you inside."

"No," she said, surprised at how vehement she felt about returning to the reception hall and the newlyweds. "I don't want to go back there."

"But—"

"Stay with me here. Dance with me. Hold me." He'd said he wanted to take care of her. Well, she was giving him the opportunity. She leaned her body into his and sighed, savoring his strength and support. This was Luke. Luke Rivers. Her trusted friend. Surely he understood; surely he would help her through this most difficult night of her life. "I want you with me." She couldn't explain what was happening between them any more than she could deny it.

"You don't know what you're asking me." He stared down at her, searching her features for a long, breathless moment. Then the cool tips of his fingers brushed her face, moving along her cheekbones, stroking her ivory skin as if he expected her to vanish.

Kate caught his hand with her own and recklessly gazed into his dark eyes. They glittered like freshly polished onyx, full of light and a deep inner fire.

"I want you to kiss me. You taste so good." She moistened her lips and leaned closer to him, so close that she could feel the imprint of his buttons against her body. So close that the beat of his heart merged with her own. Excitement shivered through her in tremors so intense they frightened her. But not enough to make her pull away.

Her words spurred Luke into action, and when he kissed her their lips met with hungry insistence. Sensation erupted between them until Kate was weak and dizzy, forced to cling to him for support, her fingers bunching the material of his jacket. When he lifted his head, ending the kiss, Kate felt nearly faint from the rush of blood to her pounding temples.

There was a look of shock on Luke's face. His eyes questioned her, but Kate's thoughts were as scattered as autumn leaves tossed by a brisk wind.

"How much champagne have you had?" he demanded softly.

"One glass," she answered with a sigh, resting her forehead against his heaving chest. Luke hadn't said taking care of her would be this wonderful. Had she known, she wouldn't have resented it quite so much earlier.

Luke expelled a harsh breath. "You've had more than one glass. I doubt you even know who I am."

"Of course I do!" she flared. "You're Luke. Now don't be ridiculous. Only..."

"Only what?"

"Only you never kissed me before. At least not like that. Why in heaven's name didn't you tell me you were so good at this?" Finding herself exceptionally witty, she began to laugh.

"I'm taking you home," Luke said firmly, grabbing her elbow with such force that she was half-lifted from the walkway.

"Luke," she cried, "I don't want to go back yet."

His grip relaxed immediately. "Kate Logan, I think you're drunk! Only you don't have the sense to know it."

"I most certainly am not!" She waved her index finger at him like a schoolmarm. "I'll have you know that it takes a lot more than one glass of champagne to do me in."

Luke obviously wasn't willing to argue the point. His hand cradling her elbow, he led her toward the parking lot.

"I want to stay," she protested.

He didn't answer. Then it dawned on her that perhaps she'd misread Luke. Maybe he wanted to be rid of her so he could return to Betty.

"Luke?"

"Kate, please, don't argue with me."

"Are you in love with Betty?"

"No." His answer was clipped and impatient.

"Thank heaven." Her hand fluttered over her heart. "I don't think I could bear it if you were."

Luke stopped abruptly and Kate realized they were standing in front of his truck. He opened the passenger door for her, but she had no intention of climbing in. At least not yet. She wanted to spend more time with Luke, their arms wrapped around each other the way they'd been before. The pain that had battered her heart for weeks had vanished the instant she stepped into his arms.

"I want you to kiss me again, okay?"

"Kate, no."

"Please?"

"Kate, you're drunk."

"And I tell you I'm not." The one glass of champagne had been just enough to make her a little... reckless. It felt so good to surrender to these new emotions—to lean on Luke. From the moment they'd arrived at the wedding, he'd been telling her how much she needed him. Maybe he was right. There'd been so much upheaval in her life, and Luke was here, warm and kind and solid.

"I'm going to drive you home," he insisted. From the sound of his voice, Kate could tell he was growing frustrated.

The house would be dark and cold. How Kate feared being alone, and with Clay out of her life, there was only her father. And Luke. If Devin did decide to marry Mrs. Murphy, he might sell the ranch and then Luke would be gone, too. Alarmed at the thought, she placed her hands on his shoulders, her gaze holding his.

"Kate?" Luke coaxed softly.

"All right, I'll go back to the house, but on one condition."

"Kate, come on, be reasonable."

"I want you to do something for me. You keep telling me you're my friend and how much you want to help...."

"Just get inside the truck, would you, before someone comes along and finds us arguing?"

"I need your promise first."

Luke ignored her. "You've got a reputation to uphold. You can't let people in Nightingale see you tipsy. The school board will hear about this and that'll be the end of your career."

Kate smiled, shaking her head, then impulsively leaned forward and kissed him again. Being with Luke took the hurt away, and she didn't want to suffer that kind of pain ever again. "Will you kindly do what I want?"

"All right," he cried, clearly exasperated. "What is it?"

"Oh, good," she murmured, and sighed expressively. This was going to shock him, but no more than it had already shocked her. She didn't know where the idea had come from, but it seemed suddenly, unarguably right.

Kate smiled at him, her heart shining through her eyes. "It's simple really. All I want you to do is marry me."

CHAPTER TWO

EARLY THE FOLLOWING DAY, Devin Logan walked hesitantly into the kitchen where Kate sat drinking her first cup of coffee. She smiled a greeting. "Morning, Dad."

"Morning, Princess." He circled the table twice before he sat down.

Kate watched him curiously, then rose to pour him a cup of coffee and deliver it to the table. It was a habit she'd begun after her mother's death several years earlier.

"Did you and Mrs. Murphy have a good time last night?" Kate asked, before her father could comment on the rumors that were sure to be circulating about her and Luke Rivers. She hadn't seen Luke yet, but she would soon enough, and she was mentally bracing herself for the confrontation. What a fool she'd made of herself. She cringed at the thought of her marriage proposal and didn't doubt for a second that Luke was going to take a good deal of delight in tormenting her about it. She suspected it would be a good long while before he let her live this one down.

"Looks like rain," Devin mumbled.

Kate grinned good-naturedly, wondering at her father's strange mood. "I asked you about last night, not about the weather."

Devin's eyes flared briefly with some unnamed emotion, which he quickly disguised. His gaze fell to the steaming mug cupped in his hands.

"Dad? Did you and Mrs. Murphy enjoy yourselves?"

"Why, sure, we had a grand time," he said with forced enthusiasm.

Knowing her father well, Kate waited for him to elaborate. Instead he reached for the sugar bowl and resolutely added three heaping teaspoons to his coffee. He stirred it so briskly the coffee threatened to slosh over the edge of his mug. All the while, he stared blankly into space.

Kate didn't know what to make of Devin's unusual behavior. "Dad," she said, trying once more, "is there something on your mind?"

His eyes darted about the room, reluctantly settling on Kate. "What makes you ask that?"

"You just added sugar to your coffee. You've been drinking it sugarless for forty years."

He glared down at the mug, surprise written on his tanned face. "I did?"

"I saw you myself."

"I did," he repeated firmly, as if that was what he'd intended all along. "I, ah, seem to have developed a sweet tooth lately."

It was becoming apparent to Kate that her father's experience at Clay's and Rorie's wedding reception must have rivaled her own. "Instead of beating around the bush all morning, why don't you just tell me what's on your mind?"

Once more, her father lowered his eyes, then nodded and swallowed tightly. "Dorothea and I had . . . a long talk last night," he began haltingly. "It all started out innocently enough. Then again, I'm sure the wedding and all the good feelings floating around Clay and Rorie probably had a good deal to do with it." He hesitated long enough to take a sip of his coffee. Grimacing at its sweetness. "The best I can figure, we started talking seriously after Nellie Jackson came by and told Dorothea and me that we made a handsome couple. At least that's how I think the conversation got started."

"It's true," Kate said kindly. Personally she would have preferred her father to see someone who resembled her mother a bit more, but Mrs. Murphy was a pleasant, gentle woman and Kate was fond of her.

Her father smiled fleetingly. "Then the champagne was passed around and Dorothea and I helped ourselves." He paused, glancing at Kate as if that explained everything.

"Yes," Kate said, hiding a smile, "go on."

Slowly Devin straightened, and eyes, forthright and unwavering, held hers. "You know I loved your mother. When Nora died, there was a time I wondered if I could go on living without her, but I have, and so have you."

"Of course you have, Dad." Suddenly it dawned on Kate exactly where this conversation was leading. It shouldn't have surprised her, and yet . . . Kate's heart was beginning to hammer uncomfortably. Her father didn't need to say another word; she knew what was coming as surely as if he'd already spoken the words aloud. He was going to marry Dorothea Murphy.

"Your mother's been gone nearly five years now and, well, a man gets lonely," her father continued. "I've been thinking about doing some traveling and, frankly, I don't want to do it alone."

"You should have said something earlier, Dad," Kate interjected. "I'd have loved traveling with you. Still would. That's one of the nice things about being a schoolteacher," she rambled on. "My summers are free. And with Luke watching the ranch, you wouldn't have any worries about what's happening at home and—"

"Princess." His spoon made an irritating clicking sound against the sides of the ceramic mug, but he didn't seem to notice. "I asked Dorothea to marry me last night and she's graciously consented."

After only a moment's hesitation, Kate found the strength to smile and murmur, "Why, Dad, that's fantastic."

"I know it's going to be hard on you, Princess—so soon after Clay's wedding and all. I want you to know that I have no intention of abandoning you—you'll always be my little girl."

"Of course you aren't abandoning me." Tears edged their way into the corners of Kate's eyes and a cold numbness moved out from her heart and spread through her body. "I'm happy for you. Really happy." She meant it, too, but she couldn't help feeling a sense of impending loss. All the emotional certainties seemed to be disappearing from her life.

Her father gently squeezed her hand. "There are going to be some other changes, as well, I'm afraid. I'm selling the ranch."

Kate gasped before she could stop herself. He'd just confirmed all her fears. She'd lost Clay to another woman, now she was about to lose her father, and her home, too. Then another thought crystallized in her mind, although that had been half formed the night before. If the ranch was sold, Luke would be gone, too.

Clay. Her father. The Circle L. Luke. Everyone and everything she loved, gone in a matter of hours. It was almost more than she could absorb at one time. Pressing her hand over her mouth, she blinked back the blinding tears.

"Now I don't want you to concern yourself," her father hurried to add. "You'll always have a home with me. Dorothea and I talked it over and we both want you to feel free to live with us in town as long as you like. You'll always be my Princess, and Dorothea understands that."

"Dad," Kate muttered, laughing and crying at the same time, unable to decide which was most appropriate. "That's ridiculous. I'm twenty-four years old and perfectly capable of living on my own."

"Of course you are, but—"

She stopped him by raising her hand. "There's no need to discuss it further. You and Dorothea Murphy are going to be married, and . . . I couldn't be happier for you. Now, don't you worry about me. I'll find a place of my own in town and make arrangements to move as soon as I can."

Her father sighed, clearly relieved by her easy acceptance of his plans, "Well, Princess," he said, shaking his head, his smile so bright it rivaled a July sun, "I can't tell you how pleased I am. Frankly, I was worried you'd be upset."

"Oh, Dad . . ."

Still grinning broadly, Devin stroked the side of his jaw. "Dorothea isn't a bit like your mother—I don't know if you noticed that or not. Fact is, the only reason I asked her out that first time was so she'd invite me over for some of her peach cobbler. Then before I knew it, I was making excuses to get into town and it wasn't because of her cobbler, either.''

Kate made an appropriate reply although a minute later she wasn't sure what she'd said. Soon afterward, her father kissed her cheek and then left the house, telling her he'd be back later that afternoon.

After her father left, Kate poured herself a second cup of coffee and leaned her hip against the kitchen counter, trying to digest everything that was happening to her well-organized life. She felt as though her whole world had been uprooted and tossed about—as though the winds of a hurricane had landed in Nightingale and swept away all that was good in her life.

Wandering aimlessly from room to room, she paused in front of the bookcase, where a photograph of her mother rested. Tears blurred her eyes as she picked it up and clutched it to her chest. Wave upon wave of emotion swept through her, followed by a flood of hot tears.

She relived the overwhelming grief she'd felt at her mother's death, and she was furious with her father for letting another woman take Nora's place in his life. At the same time, she couldn't find it in her heart to begrudge him his new happiness.

Mrs. Murphy wasn't the type of woman Kate would have chosen for her father, but then she wasn't doing the choosing. Suddenly resolute, Kate dragged in a deep breath, exhaling the fear and uncertainty and inhaling the acceptance of this sudden change in both their lives.

The back door opened and instinctively Kate closed her eyes, mentally composing herself. It could only be

Luke, and he was the last person she wanted to see right now.

"Kate?"

With trembling hands, she replaced the faded photograph and wiped the tears from her face. "Good morning, Luke," she said softly, as she entered the kitchen.

Luke had walked over to the cupboard and taken down a mug. "Your father just told me the news about him and Mrs. Murphy," he said carefully. "Are you going to be all right?"

"Of course. It's wonderful for Dad, isn't it?"

"For your father yes, but it must be something of a shock to you so soon..."

"After Clay and Rorie," she finished for him. Reaching for the coffeepot, she poured his cup and refilled her own. "I'm going to be just fine," she repeated, but Kate didn't know whether she was telling him this for his benefit or her own. "Naturally, the fact that Dad's marrying Dorothea means a few changes in all our lives, but I'll adjust."

"I haven't seen your father this happy in years."

Kate did her best to smile through the pain. "Yes, I know." To her horror tears formed again, and she lowered her gaze and blinked wildly in an effort to hide them.

"Kate?"

She whirled around and set her coffee aside while she started wiping invisible crumbs from the perfectly clean kitchen counter.

Luke's hands settled on her shoulders, and before she knew what was happening, Kate had turned and buried her face against his clean-smelling denim shirt. A single sob shook her shoulders and she heaved out a quivering sigh, embarrassed to be breaking down in front of him like this.

"Go on, baby," he whispered gently, his hands rubbing her back, "let it out."

She felt like such a weakling to be needing Luke so much, but he was so strong and steady, and Kate felt as helpless as a rowboat tossed about an angry sea. Even if she lasted through the storm, she didn't know if she could survive.

"Did . . . did you know Dad might sell the ranch?" she asked Luke.

"Yes." His voice was tight. "When did he tell you?"

"This morning, after he said he was marrying Mrs. Murphy."

"You don't need to worry about it."

"But I do," she said, and sobbed softly. She felt Luke's chin caress the crown of her head and she snuggled closer into his warm, safe embrace. Luke was her most trusted friend. He'd seen her through the most difficult day of her life.

The thought of Clay and Rorie's wedding flashed into her mind, and with it came the burning memory of her marriage proposal to Luke. She stiffened in his arms, mortified at the blatant way she'd used him, the way she'd practically begged him to take care of her— to marry her. Breaking free of his arms she straightened and offered him a watery smile.

"What would I do without you, Luke Rivers?"

"You won't ever need to find that out." He looped his arms around her waist and gently kissed the tip of her nose. His smile was tender. "There must have been something in the air last night. First us, and now your father and Mrs. Murphy."

"About us," she began carefully. She drew in a steadying breath, but her eyes avoided Luke's. "I hope you realize when I asked you to marry me that I . . . didn't actually mean it."

He went very still and for a long moment he said nothing. "I took you seriously, Kate."

Kate freed herself from his arms and reached for her coffee, gripping the mug tightly. "I'd had too much champagne."

"According to you, it was only one glass."

"Yes, but I drank it on an empty stomach, and with the difficult emotions the wedding brought out and everything, I simply wasn't myself."

Luke frowned. "Oh?"

"No, I wasn't," she said, feigning a light laugh. "The way we were dancing and the way I clung to you, and . . . and kissed you. That's nothing like me. I'm not going to hold you to that promise, Luke."

As if he found it difficult to remain standing, Luke twisted around the rail-back chair and straddled it with familiar ease. Kate claimed the chair opposite him, grateful to sit down. Her nerves were stretched to the breaking point. For several minutes Luke said nothing. He draped his forearms over the back of the chair, cupping the hot mug with both hands, and studied Kate with an intensity that made her blush.

"Listen," Kate said hesitantly, "you were the perfect gentleman and I want you to know how much I appreciate everything you did to help me. But . . . I'm afraid I didn't mean half of what I said."

The sun-marked crow's feet at the corners of his eyes fanned out as Luke smiled slowly, confidently. "Now that raises some interesting questions."

"I don't think I understand." Surely Luke knew what she was talking about, yet he seemed to enjoy watching her make an even bigger fool of herself by forcing her to explain.

"Well," he said in an easy drawl, "if you only meant half of what you said, then it leads me to wonder what you did mean and what you didn't."

"I can't remember *everything* I said," she murmured, her cheeks hot enough to pop a batch of corn. "But I do know I'd greatly appreciate it if you'd forget the part about marrying me."

"I don't want to forget it."

"Luke, please," she cried, squeezing her eyes shut. "This is embarrassing me. Couldn't you kindly drop it?"

Luke rubbed his jaw thoughtfully. "I don't think I can."

So Luke was going to demand his pound of flesh. Kate supposed she shouldn't be so surprised. She had, after all, brought this on herself. "You were so good to me at the reception... After the wedding ceremony you kept saying that you wanted to help me and, Luke, you did, you honestly did. I don't think I could have made it through Clay's wedding without you, but..."

"You want to forget the kissing, too?"

"Yes, please." She nodded emphatically.

He frowned. "That's not what you said last night. In fact, you were downright surprised at how pleasant it was. As I recall you told me—and I quote—'why in heaven's name didn't you tell me you were so good at this?'"

"Dear Lord, I said that?" Kate muttered, already knowing it was true.

"I'm afraid so."

She covered her face with both hands as the hot color mounted in her cheeks.

"And you practically forced me to promise I'd marry you."

She bit down hard on her lower lip. "Anyone else in the world would have mercifully forgotten I suggested that."

With a certain amount of ceremony, Luke set his hat farther back on his head and folded his arms. His face was a study in concentration. "I have no intention of forgetting it. I'm a man of my word and I never break my promises."

Kate groaned. In light of her father's news this morning, she'd hoped Luke might be a little more understanding. "It's obvious you're deriving a good deal of pleasure from all this," she muttered angrily, and then pressed her lips together to keep from saying more.

"No, not exactly. When would you like to have the wedding? And while we're at it, you might as well find out now that—"

"You can't be serious!" she interrupted, incredulous that he'd suggest they set a date. If this was a joke, he was carrying it too far.

"I'm dead serious. You asked me to marry you, I agreed, and anything less would be a breach of good faith."

"Then I . . . I absolve you from your promise." She waved her hands as if she was granting some kind of formal dispensation.

He stroked the side of his face, his forehead creased in a contemplative frown. "My word is my word and I stand firm on it."

"I didn't know what I was saying—well, I did. Sort of. But you know as well as I do that the…heat of the moment was doing most of the talking."

Luke's frown deepened. "I suppose everybody in town will assume you're marrying me on the rebound. Either that, or I'll be the one they'll gossip about. That doesn't trouble me much, but I don't like the thought of folks saying anything about you."

"Will you kindly stop?" she cried. "I have no intention of marrying anyone! Ever!" She was finished with love, finished with romance. Thirty years from now she'd be living alone with a few companion cats and her knitting needles.

"That wasn't what you said last night."

"Would you quit saying that? I wasn't myself, for heaven's sake!"

"Well, our getting married sounded like a hell of a good idea to me. Now, I realize you've gone through a hard time, but our marriage will end all that."

Kate brushed a shaking hand across her eyes, hoping this scene was just part of a nightmare and she'd soon wake up. Unfortunately when she lowered her hand, Luke was still sitting there, as arrogant as could be. "I can't believe we're even having this discussion. It's totally unreasonable, and if you're trying to improve my mood, you've failed."

"I'm serious, Kate. I already explained that."

Keeping her head down, she spoke quickly, urgently. "It's really wonderful of you to even consider going through with the marriage, but it isn't necessary, Luke. More than anyone, you should understand that I can't marry you. Not when I love Clay Franklin the way I do."

"Hogwash."

Kate's head jerked up. "I beg your pardon?"

"You're in love with me. You just don't know it yet."

It took Kate only half a second to respond. "Of all the egotistical, vain, high-handed . . ." She paused to suck in a breath. If Luke's intent was to shock her, he'd succeeded. "I can't believe you!" She bolted to her feet and flailed the air with both hands. Unable to stand still, she started pacing the kitchen. "I don't understand you. I've tried, honestly I've tried. One moment you're the Rock of Gibraltar, steady and secure and everything I need, my best friend, and the next moment you're saying the most ridiculous things to me. It never used to be this way between us! What happened? Why have you changed?"

"Is it really that bad?" he cajoled softly, ignoring her questions.

"I don't know what happened to you—to us—at the wedding reception, but obviously something must have been in the air. Let's attribute it to the champagne and drop it before one of us ends up getting hurt."

"You know, if you gave the idea of our getting married some serious thought, it might grow on you," he suggested next.

Then he got to his feet and moved purposefully toward her. His mouth twisted into a cocky grin. "Maybe this will help you decide what's best."

"I—"

He laid a finger across her mouth to stop her. "It seems to me you've forgotten it's not ladylike to be quite so stubborn." With that, he slipped his arm around her waist and gently pulled her against him.

Knowing what he intended, Kate opened her mouth to protest, but he fastened his lips over hers, sealing off the words, and to her chagrin, soon erasing them altogether. Her fingers gripped the collar of his blue button-snap shirt and against every dictate of her will, her mouth parted willingly, welcoming his touch.

When he released her, it was a minor miracle that she didn't collapse on the floor. He paused and a wide grin split his face.

"Yup," he said, looking more than pleased, "you love me all right."

CHAPTER THREE

KATE HAD NEVER FELT more grateful for a Monday morning than she did the following day. At least when she was at school, she had the perfect excuse to avoid another confrontation with Luke. He seemed to believe he was somehow responsible for her and to take that responsibility quite seriously. She had no intention of holding him to his promise and couldn't understand why he was being so stubborn. To suggest she was in love with him simply because she'd proposed marriage and responded ardently to his kisses revealed how truly irrational Luke Rivers had become.

Kate paused and let that thought run through her mind once more, then laughed aloud. No wonder Luke insisted on marrying her. Kate had to admit she could see why he might have the wrong impression. Still, she wished she could think of some way to set him straight.

Luke was right about a few things, though. She *did* love him—but not the way he implied. She felt for him as a sister does toward a special older brother. As a woman does toward a confidant and companion of many years' standing. The feelings she'd experienced when he kissed her were something of a mystery, but could easily be attributed to the heightened emotions following Clay's wedding. So much had been going on in Kate's life the past few months that she barely understood herself anymore.

She could never love Luke the way she had Clay. For as long as Kate could remember, she'd pictured herself as Clay's wife. Linking her life with any other man's seemed not only wrong but completely foreign.

"Good morning, Miss Logan," seven-year-old Taylor Morgenroth said as he casually strolled into the classroom. "I saw you at Mr. Franklin's wedding on Saturday."

"You did?" It shouldn't surprise her, since nearly every family in town had been represented at the wedding. Probably more than one of her students had seen her.

"You were with Mr. Rivers, weren't you? My mom kept asking my dad who you were dancing with. That was Mr. Rivers, wasn't it?"

"Yes." Kate had to bite her tongue to keep from explaining that she hadn't actually been "with" Luke. He wasn't her official date, although they'd attended the wedding together. But explaining something like that to a second-grader would only confuse the child.

"My dad made me dance with my older sister. It was yucky."

Kate managed to mumble something about how much of a gentleman Taylor had been, but she doubted that he wanted to hear it.

Before long, the students of Nightingale Elementary were eagerly filing into the classroom and rushing toward their desks. From that point on, Kate didn't have time to think about Luke or Saturday night or anything else except her lesson plans for the day.

At noon she took her brown-bag lunch to the faculty lounge. Several of the other teachers were already seated at the circular tables.

"Kate!" Sally Daley, the sixth-grade teacher, waved her hand to gain Kate's attention. She smiled, patting the empty chair beside her.

Reluctantly Kate joined the older woman, sending an apologetic look to her friend Linda Hutton, the third-grade teacher, whom she usually joined for lunch. Sally had the reputation of being a busybody, but Kate couldn't think of a way to avoid her without being rude.

"We were just talking about you," Sally said warmly, "and we thought it would be nice if you'd sit with us today."

"I'll be happy to," Kate said, feeling a twinge of guilt at the lie. She opened her brown bag, taking out a container of peach-flavored yogurt and two rye crisps.

"Clay's wedding was really lovely, wasn't it?" Sally asked without any preamble. "And now I understand your father and Dorothea Murphy are going to be tying the knot?" Her questioning tone indicated she wasn't certain of her facts.

"That's right," Kate said cheerfully.

"Kind of a surprise, wasn't it?"

"Kind of," was all Kate would admit, although now she realized she should have known her father was falling in love with Mrs. Murphy. They'd been spending more and more time together since early summer. If Kate hadn't been so blinded by what was happening between her and Clay, she would have noticed how serious her father had become about Dorothea long before now.

"It's going to be difficult for you, isn't it, dear?" Sally asked sympathetically. "Everyone knows how close you and your father have been since Nora died."

"I'm very pleased my father's going to remarry." And Kate was. The initial shock had worn off; she felt genuinely and completely happy that her father had found someone to love. He'd never complained, but Kate knew he'd been lonely during the past few years.

"Still it must be something of a blow," Sally pressed, "especially following on the heels of Clay and Rorie getting married? It seems your whole life has been turned upside down of late, doesn't it?"

Kate nodded, keeping her eyes focused on her sparse meal.

"Speaking of Clay and Rorie, their wedding was exceptionally lovely."

"I thought so, too," Kate said, smiling through the pain. "Rorie will make him a perfect wife." The words nearly stuck in her throat, although she was fully aware of their truth. Rorie was an ideal complement to Clay. From the moment she'd stepped into their lives, she'd obviously belonged with Clay.

"The new Mrs. Franklin is certainly an ambitious soul. Why the library hasn't been the same since she took over. There are education programs going on there every other week. Displays. Lectures. I tell you, nothing but good has happened since she moved to Nightingale."

"I couldn't agree with you more."

Sally looked pleased. "I think you've taken this . . . disappointment over Clay rather well," she murmured with cloying sympathy. "And now your father remarrying so soon afterward..." She gently patted Kate's hand. "If there's anything I can do for you, Kate, anything at all, during this difficult time, I don't want you to hesitate to call me. I know I speak for each and every staff member when I say that. Your father must see you've been a wonderful daughter, and I'm sorry all of this is being heaped on your shoulders just now. But if it's ever more than you can bear, your friends at Nightingale Elementary will be honored to stand at your side. All you have to do is call."

If Sally was expecting a lengthy response, Kate couldn't manage it. "Thank you. That's...really wonderful to know," she said in a faltering voice. To hear Sally tell it, Kate was close to a nervous breakdown.

"We're prepared to stand at your side as you pick up the shattered pieces of your life. And furthermore, I think Luke Rivers is a fine man."

"Luke Rivers?" Kate repeated, nearly choking on her bite of rye crisp. A huge knot formed in her throat at Sally's implication.

"Why, yes." Sally paused and smiled serenely. "Everyone in Nightingale saw how the two of you were gazing into each other's eyes at the dance. It was the most romantic thing I've seen in years."

"Dance?"

"At the wedding-reception dance," Sally elaborated. "From what I understand, Betty Hammond's been so depressed she hasn't left her house since that night."

"Whatever for?"

Sally laughed lightly. "Surely there's no reason to be so reticent—you're among friends. Everyone knows how Betty's had her eye on Luke for years.

From what I understand they dated a couple of times a year or so ago, but Luke's kept her dangling ever since.''

"I don't have a clue what you mean," Kate said faintly, her heart beating hard enough to pound its way out of her chest. She'd hoped that with her father's engagement, the rumors about her and Luke would naturally fade away. So much for wishful thinking.

Sally exchanged a meaningful look with her friends. "Well, I thought that, you know…that you and Luke Rivers had a thing going."

"Luke and me?" Kate gave a short, almost hysterical laugh. "Nothing could be further from the truth. Luke's a dear friend, and we've known each other for years, but we're not romantically involved. There's nothing between us. Absolutely nothing." She spoke more vehemently than necessary, feeling pleased that for once Sally couldn't manage a single word.

After a moment, she made a show of looking at her watch. "Excuse me, ladies, but I've got to get back to my classroom."

As she left the faculty lounge, she heard the whispers start. Groaning inwardly, Kate marched down the hall and into her own room. Sitting at her desk, she snapped the cracker in half and examined it closely before tossing it into the garbage.

"Don't you know it's wrong to waste food?" Linda Hutton said, leaning against the doorjamb, arms folded.

"I wished I'd never talked to that woman," Kate muttered, feeling foolish for allowing herself to be manipulated into conversation with a known busybody.

"Well, then," Linda said, with a knowing grin, "why did you?"

"If I knew the answer to that, I'd be enjoying my lunch instead of worrying about the tales Sally's going to spread all over town about me...and Luke Rivers."

Linda walked nonchalantly into the room.

"The least you could have done was rescue me," Kate complained.

"Hey, I leave that kind of work to the fire department." Linda leaned forward and planted her hands on the edge of Kate's desk. "Besides, I was curious myself."

"You're curious about what? Luke and me? Honestly, all we did was dance a couple of times. I...was feeling warm and went outside for a little bit. Luke met me there and after a few minutes, he...drove me home. What's the big deal, anyway?"

"A couple of dances...I see," Linda said, her words slow and thoughtful.

"I'd be interested in knowing exactly what you see. Everyone keeps making an issue of the dancing. Taylor came into class this morning and the first thing he mentioned was that he'd seen me at the wedding. He didn't talk about running into me at the grocery store earlier that same day."

"Did you have your arms wrapped around a man there, too?"

"Don't be silly!"

"I wasn't. Honestly, Kate, nearly everyone in Nightingale saw the way you and Luke were dancing. You acted as though there wasn't anyone else at the reception. Needless to say, rumors were floating in every direction. Everyone was watching the two of you, and neither you or Luke even noticed. Or cared. I heard the pastor mumble something about the possibility of performing another wedding soon, and he wasn't referring to your father and Dorothea Murphy—which is something else entirely.'' Linda paused to suck in a deep breath. ''Are you sure you're going to be able to handle this on top of—''

''Clay and Rorie? Yes,'' Kate answered her own question emphatically. ''Oh, I had a few bad moments when Dad first told me, but I got over it.'' The comfort she'd found in Luke's arms had helped her more than she cared to admit. He seemed to be making a habit of helping her through difficult moments.

Linda eyed her skeptically. ''There's been so much upheaval in your life these past few weeks. You know sometimes people go into shock for weeks after a major change in their lives.''

''Linda,'' Kate cried, ''everyone keeps looking at me as though they expect me to have a nervous breakdown or something. What is it with you people?''

''It isn't us, Katie girl, it's you.''

Kate pushed her hair off her forehead and kept her hand pressed there. ''What do I have to do to convince you that I'm fine? I'm happy for Clay and Rorie. I like to think of myself as resilient and emotionally strong, but it makes me wonder why you and Sally and the others don't.''

''I don't think anyone's waiting for you to fall apart,'' Linda countered. ''We all have your best interests at heart. In fact with one obvious exception, everyone's really pleased you have Luke.''

''But I don't *have* him. Luke isn't a possession, he's a man. We're friends. You know that.'' She expected Linda, of all her friends and colleagues, to recognize the truth when she heard it. Instead she'd made it sound as though Kate's dancing with Luke and then letting him take her home early meant instant wedding bells.

Linda took a moment to consider her answer. "To be honest, Kate, you're doing a whole lot of denying and I don't understand why. It seems to me that the person you're most trying to convince is yourself."

By the time Kate arrived home that evening, she was in a fine temper. Her father had already left for a meeting at the Eagles Lodge. He'd taped a note to the refrigerator door telling her not to worry about fixing him any dinner because he planned to stop off at Dorothea's for a bite to eat later.

Kate read his scrawled note, pulled it off the fridge and crumpled it with both hands. She was angry and impatient for no reason she could identify.

Heating herself a bowl of soup, Kate stood in front of the stove stirring it briskly when Luke let himself in the back door. After her encounter with Sally and Linda, Luke was the last person she wanted to see that evening. Nevertheless, her eyes flew anxiously to his.

"Evening, Kate."

"Hi."

He hung his hat on the peg next to the door, then walked to the kitchen counter and examined the empty soup can. "I hope you're going to eat more than this."

"Luke," she said, slowly expelling her breath. "I had a terrible day and I'm rotten company."

"What happened?"

Kate didn't want to talk about it. Dredging up her lunch-hour conversation with Sally Daley would only refuel her unhappiness.

"Kate?" Luke coaxed.

She shrugged. "The other teachers heard about Dad and Dorothea and seemed to think the shock would do me in, if you know what I mean."

"I think I do." As he was speaking, he took two bowls out of the cupboard and set them on the table.

Kate stirred the soup energetically, not looking at him, almost afraid of his reaction. "In addition, people are talking about us."

When she glanced in his direction, Luke nodded, his eyes twinkling. "I thought they might be."

"I don't like it!" she burst out. The least Luke could do was show the proper amount of concern. "Sally Daley told me how pleased she was with the way I'd rebounded from a broken heart." She paused, waiting for his response. When he didn't give her one, she added, "Sally seems to think you and I are perfect together."

Luke grinned. "And that upset you?"

"Yes!" she cried.

"Sally didn't mean anything. She's got a big heart."

"Her mouth is even bigger," Kate retorted. "We're in trouble here, Luke Rivers, and I want to know exactly how we're going to get out of it."

"The answer to that is simple. We should get married and put an end to speculation."

Kate's shoulders sagged in defeat. "Luke, please, I'm just not in the mood for your teasing tonight. The time has come for us to get serious about..."

Her voice dwindled as Luke, standing behind her, placed his hands on her shoulders and nuzzled her neck. "I'm willing."

His touch had a curious effect on Kate's senses, which seemed to leap to life. It took every ounce of fortitude she possessed to resist melting into his arms and accepting his gentle comfort. But that was how they'd got into this mess in the first place.

"The gossips are having a field day and I hate it."

Luke drew her away from the stove and turned her toward him. He searched her face, but his own revealed not a hint of annoyance or distress. "I don't mind if folks talk. It's only natural, don't you think?"

"How can you say that?" This whole situation with Luke had complctcly unnerved her, while he seemed to take it in his stride.

"Kate, you're making this out to be some kind of disaster."

"But don't you see? It is! There are people out there who honestly believe we're falling in love."

"You do love me. I told you that earlier. Remember?"

"Oh, Luke," she cried, so disheartened she wanted to weep. "I understand what you're trying to do and I appreciate it with all my heart, but it isn't necessary. It really isn't."

Luke looked baffled. "I don't think I understand."

"You've been such a dear." She laid her hand against his clean-shaven cheek. "Any other man would have laughed in my face when I made him promise to marry me, but you agreed and now, out of consideration for *my* pride, *my* feelings, you claim you're going to go through with it."

"Kate," he said, guiding her to the table and gently pressing her into a chair. "Sit down. I have something important to tell you—something I've been trying to tell you since the night of the wedding."

"What is it?" she asked, once she was seated.

Luke paced the floor directly in front of her chair, frowning deeply. "I should have told you much sooner, but with everything else that's going on in your life, finding the right time has been difficult." He paused in his pacing and looked at her as though he was having trouble finding the words.

"Yes?" she coaxed.

"I'm buying the Circle L."

The kitchen started to sway. Kate reached out and gripped the edge of the table. She'd hoped it would be several months before a buyer could be found. And it had never occurred to her that Luke might be that buyer. "I see," she said, smiling through her shock. "I . . . I'd have thought Dad would've said something himself."

"I asked him not to."

Her troubled gaze clashed with Luke's. Despite her shock she felt curious. How could Luke afford to buy a ranch, especially one as large as this? She knew he'd been raised by an uncle, who had died years before. Had there been an inheritance? "Luke," she ventured shyly, "I know it's none of my business, but..."

"How did I come by the money?" he finished for her. "You have every right to ask, Princess. I inherited it from my Uncle Dan—I've told you about him. He owned a couple of businesses in Wyoming, where I grew up. There was a small sum left to me by my grandfather. I invested everything, together with most of what Devin's paid me over the years, and I've got enough now to buy the ranch outright—which'll leave your dad and Dorothea in good financial shape for their retirement. I'll be able to expand the operation, too."

Kate nodded absently. She hadn't known much about Luke's background, apart from the fact that he had very little family, that he'd lost his parents at an early age. She supposed those losses were the reason he'd been so sympathetic, such a comfort to her and Devin, at the time of Nora's death.

It still seemed too much to take in. Her home—it was going to belong to Luke. He'd move his things from the small foreman's house, though she knew he hadn't accumulated many possessions. But it meant that soon she would be sorting through and packing up the memories of a lifetime.... She frowned and bit her lip.

He knelt in front of her, gripping her fingers with his warm, hard hands. "I realize you've been through a lot of emotional upheaval lately, but this should help."

"Help!" she wailed. "How could it possibly—"

"There isn't any reason for you to be uprooted now."

For a stunned second she didn't react. "I don't have the slightest idea what you're talking about."

"Once we're married, we'll live right here."

"Married!" she almost shouted. "I'm beginning to hate the sound of that word."

"You'd best get used to it, because the way I figure it we're going to be husband and wife before Christmas. We'll let Devin and Dorothea take their vows first—I don't want to steal their thunder—and then we'll wait a couple of weeks and have the Reverend Wilkins marry us."

"Luke, this is all very sweet of you, but *it isn't necessary.*" Although he hadn't said as much, Kate was convinced that this sudden desire to make her his wife was founded in sympathy. He felt sorry for her, because of all the unexpected jolts that had hit her recently. Including this latest one.

"I can't understand why you're arguing with me."

Her hand caressed his jaw. How square and strong it was, and the eyes that gazed at her had never seemed darker or more magnetic. She smiled sadly. "Don't you think it's a little . . . odd to be discussing marriage when you've never once said you loved me?"

"I love you."

Despite the seriousness of the moment, Kate laughed. "Oh, honestly, Luke, that was terrible."

"I'm serious. I love you and you love me."

"Of course we love each other, but what we feel is what *friends* feel. The kind of love brothers and sisters share."

Fire leapt into his eyes, unlike anything she'd seen in him before. With any other man, she would have been frightened—but this was Luke. . . .

"Instead of looking at me as if you're tempted to toss me over your knee, you should be grateful I'm not holding you to your word."

"Kate," he said forcefully. "we're getting married." He spoke as though he were daring her to argue with him.

Gently she lowered her head and brushed his lips with her own. "No, we're not. I'll always be grateful to have had a friend as good as you, Luke Rivers. Every woman deserves someone just as kind and thoughtful, but we'd be making the biggest mistake of our lives if we went through with this marriage."

"I don't think that's true."

"I'm sane and rational and I'm not going to disintegrate under the emotional stress of Clay's wedding or my father's remarriage, or the selling of the ranch. Life goes on—I learned that after my mother died. It sounds so clichéd, but it's true. I learned to deal with losing her and I'll do the same with everything else that's been happening."

"Kate, you don't understand. I *want* to marry you."

"Oh, Luke, it's so sweet of you. But you don't love me. Not the way you should. Someday, you'll make some lucky woman a fantastic husband." Kate had grown accustomed to his comfortable presence. But while she felt at ease with him, she experienced none of the thrill, the urgent excitement, that being in love entailed.

With Clay, the intensity of emotion had wrapped itself around her so securely that she'd been certain it would last a lifetime. Kate hadn't fooled herself into believing Clay felt as strongly for her. He'd been fond of her, and Kate had been willing to settle for that. But it hadn't been enough for him. She wasn't going to allow Luke to settle for second best in his life.

"People are going to talk, so we both have to do our best to put an end to the rumors."

"I don't intend to do any such thing," Luke said, his jaw rigid. His eyes narrowed. "Kate, darling, a marriage between us is inevitable. The sooner you accept that, the better it will be for everyone involved.

CHAPTER FOUR

"THE WAY I FIGURE IT," Kate said, munching hard on a carrot stick, "the only way to convince Luke I don't plan to marry him is to start dating someone else."

Linda looked as if she were about to swallow her apple whole. The two were seated in the school lunchroom late Friday afternoon, reviewing plans for the Thanksgiving play their two classes would present the following month.

"Start dating someone else?" Linda echoed, still wearing a stunned expression. "Not more than two days ago you announced that you were finished with love and completely opposed to the idea of men and marriage."

"I'm not looking to fall in love again," Kate explained impatiently. "That would be ridiculous."

"You talk about being ridiculous?" Linda asked, absently setting down her half-eaten apple. "We were discussing Pilgrim costume designs and suddenly you decide you want to start dating. I take it you're not referring to Miles Standish?"

"Of course not."

"That's what I thought."

Kate supposed she wasn't making a lot of sense to her friend. Luke and the issue of marriage had been on her mind all week, but she'd carefully avoided any mention of the subject. Until now. The rumors regarding her and Luke continued to burn like a forest fire through Nightingale, aided, Kate was sure, by the silly grin Luke wore about town, and the fact that he was buying her father's ranch. True, he hadn't pressured her into setting a wedding date again, but the thought was there, waiting to envelop her every time they were in the same room. She used to be able to laugh and joke with Luke, but lately, the minute they were together, Kate found herself raising her protective force field. She was beginning to feel like a character out of *Star Wars*.

"All right, you've piqued my curiosity," Linda said, her eyes flashing with humor. "Tell me about this sudden interest in the opposite sex."

"I want to stop the rumors naturally." And, she thought, convince Luke that her marriage proposal had been rooted in self-pity. He'd been so strong and she'd felt so fragile.

Linda pushed aside the pages of the Thanksgiving project notes. "Have you picked out anyone in particular?"

"No," Kate murmured, frowning. "I've been out of circulation for so long, I don't know who's available."

"No one," Linda told her in a despondent voice. "And I should know. If you want the truth, I think Nightingale would make an excellent locale for a convent. Have you ever considered the religious life?"

Kate ignored that. "Didn't I hear Sally Daley mention something about a new guy who recently moved to town? I'm sure I did and she seemed to think he was single."

"Eric Wilson. Attorney, mid-thirties, divorced, with a small mole on his left shoulder."

Kate was astonished. "Good heavens, how did Sally know all that?"

Linda shook her head slowly. "I don't even want to guess."

"Eric Wilson." Kate repeated the name slowly, letting each syllable roll off her tongue. She decided the name had a friendly feel, though it didn't really tell her anything about the man himself.

"Have you met him?" Kate asked her friend.

Linda shook her head. "No, but you're welcome to him, if you want. The only reason Sally mentioned him to me was that she assumed you and Luke would be married before the holidays were over."

A sense of panic momentarily swamped Kate. Luke had mentioned getting married around Christmas, too. "There's always Andy Barrett," Kate pointed out. Andy worked at the pharmacy, and was single. True, he wasn't exactly a heartthrob, but he was a decent-enough sort.

Linda immediately rejected that possibility. "No one in town would believe you'd choose Andy over Luke." A smile played across her mouth, as if she found the idea of Kate and Andy together somehow comical. "Andy's sweet, don't get me wrong," Linda amended, "but Luke's a real man."

"I'll think of someone," Kate murmured, her determination fierce.

Linda started to gather her Thanksgiving notes. "If you're serious about this, then you may have no choice but to import a man from Portland."

"You're kidding, I hope," Kate groaned.

"I'm dead serious," Linda said, shoving everything into her briefcase.

Her friend's words echoed depressingly through Kate's mind as she pushed her cart to the frozen-food section of the grocery store later that afternoon. She peered at the TV dinners, trying to choose something for dinner. Her father had dined with Dorothea every night since they'd become engaged, and the wedding was planned for early December.

"The beef burgundy is good," a resonant male voice said from behind her.

Kate turned to face a tall, friendly-looking man with flashing blue eyes and a lazy smile.

"Eric Wilson," he introduced himself, holding out his hand.

"Kate Logan," she said, her heart racing as they exchanged handshakes. It was all Kate could do not to mention that she'd been talking about him only minutes before and that she'd learned he was possibly the only decent single man in town—other than Luke, of course. How bizarre that they should run into each other almost immediately afterward. Perhaps not! Perhaps it was fate.

"The Salisbury steak isn't half-bad, either." As if to prove his point, he deposited both the beef burgundy and the Salisbury-steak frozen dinners in his cart.

"You sound as though you know."

"I've discovered frozen entrées are less trouble than a wife."

He frowned as he spoke, so she guessed that his divorce had been unpleasant. Sally would know, and Kate made a mental note to ask her later. She'd do so blatantly, of course, since Sally was sure to spread Kate's interest in the transplanted lawyer all over the county.

"You're new in town, aren't you? An attorney?"

Eric nodded. "At your service."

Kate was thinking fast. It had been a long time since she'd last flirted with a man. "Does that mean I can sue you if the beef burgundy isn't to my liking?"

He grinned at that, and although her comment hadn't been especially witty, she felt encouraged by his smile.

"You might have trouble getting the judge to listen to your suit, though," he told her.

"Judge Webster is my uncle," she said, laughing.

"And I suppose you're his favorite niece."

"Naturally."

"In that case, might I suggest we avoid the possibility of a lawsuit and I buy you dinner?"

That was so easy Kate couldn't believe it. She'd been out of the dating game for a long time, and she'd been sure it would take weeks to get the hang of it again. "I'd be honored."

It wasn't until Kate was home, high on her success, that she realized Eric, as a new man in town, was probably starved for companionship. That made her pride sag just a little, but she wasn't about to complain. Within hours of declaring that she wanted to start dating, she'd met a man. An attractive, pleasant man, too. It didn't matter that he'd asked her out because he was lonely or that he was obviously still licking the wounds from his divorce. A date was a date.

Kate showered and changed into a mid-calf burgundy wool skirt and a rose-colored silk blouse. She was putting the last coat of polish on her nails when her father strolled into the kitchen. Even from her position at the far side of the room, Kate caught a strong whiff of his spicy after-shave. She smiled a little.

"You look nice."

"Thanks," he said, tugging on the lapels of his tweed jacket, then brushing the sleeves.

"Do you want me to wait up for you?"

A light pink flush worked its way up Devin's neck. "Of course not."

Kate loved teasing him, and as their eyes met, they both started to laugh.

"You're looking awfully pretty yourself," Devin commented. "Are you and Luke going out?"

"Eric Wilson is taking me to dinner."

Devin regarded her quizzically. "Who? You're jesting, aren't you?"

"No." She gave him a warning frown. "Eric's new here. We met in the frozen-food section at the Safeway store this afternoon and he asked me to dinner."

"And you accepted?" His eyes were wide with astonishment.

"Of course. It beats sitting around here and watching reruns on television."

"But . . . but what about Luke?"

"What about him?"

"I thought . . . I'd hoped after Clay's wedding that the two of you might—"

"Dad, Luke's a dear friend, but we're not in love with each other."

For a moment Devin looked as if he wanted to argue, but apparently decided against it. "He's a good man, Princess."

"Trust me, I know that. If it weren't for Luke, I don't know how I would have survived the last couple of months."

"Folks in town got the impression you two might be falling in love, and I can't say I blame them after watching you at the wedding."

Kate focused her attention on polishing her nails, knowing that an identical shade of red had crept into her cheeks.

"Luke and I are friends, Dad, nothing more," she repeated.

"I don't mind letting you know, Kate, I think very highly of Luke. If I were to handpick a husband for you, it would be him."

"I . . . think Luke's wonderful, too," she said, her words faltering.

"Now that he's buying the ranch, well, it seems natural that the two of you—"

"Dad, please," she whispered. "I'm not in love with Luke, and he doesn't love me."

"That's a real pity," came Devin's softly drawled response. He reached for his hat, then paused by the door. "I don't suppose Luke knows you're going out tonight, does he?"

"There isn't any reason to tell him." She struggled to sound nonchalant. But the last thing she needed or wanted was another showdown with Luke. Pleadingly, she raised her eyes to her father. "You aren't going to tell him, are you?"

"I won't lie to him."

"Oh, no, I wouldn't expect you to do that," Kate murmured. She blew at the red polish on her nails, trying to dry them quickly. With luck Eric would arrive soon and she could make her escape before she encountered Luke.

Kate should have known that was asking too much. She was standing at the kitchen window beside the oak table, waiting for Eric's headlights to come down the long driveway, when Luke walked into the house.

Kate groaned inwardly, but said nothing. Her fingers tightened on the curtain as she changed her silent entreaty. Now she prayed that Eric would be late.

"You've got your coat on," Luke observed, as he helped himself to coffee.

"I'll be leaving in a couple of minutes," she said, hoping she didn't sound as tense as she felt. Then, a little guiltily, she added, "I baked some oatmeal cookies this afternoon. The cookie jar's full, so help yourself."

He did exactly that, then sat down at the table. "If I didn't know better, I'd think you were waiting for someone."

"I am."

"Who?"

"A...friend." Her back was to him, but Kate could feel the tension mounting in the air between them.

"Are you upset about something?"

"No. Should I be?" she asked in an offhand manner.

"You've been avoiding me all week," Luke murmured.

He was sitting almost directly behind her and Kate felt his presence acutely. Her knees were shaking, her breath coming in short, uneven gulps. She felt almost light-headed. It had to be nerves. If Luke discovered she was going to dinner with Eric there could be trouble. Yes, that explained the strange, physical reaction she was experiencing, she told herself.

"Kate, love—"

"Please," she implored, "don't call me that." She let go of the curtain and turned to face him. "I made a mistake, and considering the circumstances, it was understandable. Please, Luke, can't you drop this whole marriage business? Please?''

His look of shocked surprise didn't do anything to settle her nerves. A strained moment passed before Luke relaxed, chuckling. ''I've broken stallions who've given me less trouble than you.''

''I'm no stallion.''

Luke chuckled again, and before she could move, his arms reached out and circled her waist to pull her onto his lap.

Kate was so astonished that for a crazy moment she didn't react at all. ''Let me go,'' she said stiffly, holding her chin at a regal angle.

He ignored her demand and instead lightly ran the tips of his fingers along the side of her jaw and stroked downward to cup her chin. ''I've missed you this week, Princess.''

A trail of warmth followed his cool fingers, and a foreign sensation nibbled at her stomach. Kate didn't know what was wrong with her—and she didn't *want* to know.

''I've decided to give you a chance to think matters through before we contact Pastor Wilkins—''

''Before we what?'' she flared.

''Before we're married,'' he explained patiently, his voice much too low and seductive to suit her. ''But every time we're together, you run away like a frightened kitten.''

''Did you stop to think there might be a perfectly logical reason for that?'' She'd told him repeatedly that she wasn't going to marry him, but it didn't seem to do any good. ''I'm sorry, I truly am, but I just don't think of you in that way.''

"Oh?"

He raised his hand and threaded his fingers through her hair. She tried to pull away, to thwart him, with no effect.

"That's not the feeling I get when I kiss you."

She braced her hands against his shoulder, her fingers curling into the powerful muscles there. "I apologize if I've given you the wrong impression," she said, her voice feeble.

He cocked his brows at her statement, and his lips quivered with the effort to suppress a smile. That infuriated Kate, but she held on to her temper, knowing an argument would be pointless.

"It seems to me," he continued softly, "that we need some time alone to explore what's happening between us."

Alarm rose in Kate's throat, as she struggled to hide her response to him. The last thing she wanted was "time alone" with Luke.

"I'm afraid that's impossible tonight," she said hastily.

"Why's that?"

He was so close that his breath fanned her flushed face. It was all Kate could do to keep from closing her eyes and surrendering to the sensations that encircled her like lazy curls of smoke from a camp fire.

His mouth found her neck and he rained a long series of kisses there, each one a small dart of pleasure that robbed her of clear thought. For a wild moment, she couldn't catch her breath. His hands were in her hair, and his mouth was working its magic on her.

"No," she breathed, her voice low and trembling. Any resistance she'd managed to muster had vanished.

"Yes, my darlin' Kate."

He captured her mouth then, and excitement erupted inside her. She clung to him, her arms wrapped around his neck as his lips returned again and again to taste and tantalize her.

When he buried his face in the hollow of her throat, Kate moaned softly. She felt nearly faint from the rush of pleasure.

"Call Linda and cancel whatever plans you've made," he whispered.

Kate froze. "I can't."

"Yes, you can. I'll talk to her, if you want."

"I'm not going out with Linda." How weak she sounded.

"Then call whoever you're going out with and cancel."

"No..."

A flash of headlights through the kitchen window announced Eric's arrival. With a burst of desperate energy, Kate leapt off Luke's lap. She felt disoriented and bewildered for a moment. She rubbed her hands over her face, realizing she'd probably smudged her makeup, but that didn't concern her as much as the unreserved way she'd submitted to Luke's touch. He'd kissed her before and it had been wonderful—more than wonderful. But in those brief moments when he'd held her, at the wedding and then again the next day, she hadn't experience this burning need. It terrified her.

"Kate?"

She looked at Luke without really seeing him. "I've got to go," she insisted.

"There's a man here."

Kate opened the door for Eric. "Hi," she greeted, doing her best to appear bright and cheerful, but knowing she looked and sounded as though she was coming down with a bad case of flu. "I see you found the place without a problem."

"I had one hell of a time," he said, glancing at his watch. "Didn't you notice I'm fifteen minutes late?"

Well, no, she hadn't. Not really.

"Kate, who is this man?" Luke demanded in a steely voice.

"Eric Wilson, this is Luke Rivers. Luke is buying the Circle L," she said, hoping she didn't sound as breathless as she felt.

The two men exchanged the briefest of handshakes.

Kate didn't dare look in Luke's direction. She didn't need to, she could feel the resentment and annoyance that emanated from him like waves of heat. "Well, I suppose we should be on our way," Kate said quickly to Eric, throwing him a tight, nervous smile.

"Yes, I suppose we should." Eric's gaze traveled from Kate to Luke, then back again. He looked equally eager to make an escape.

"I'll say good-night, Luke," she said pointedly, her hand on the back door.

He didn't respond, which was just as well.

Once they were outside, Eric opened his car door for her. "You said Luke is buying the ranch?"

"Yes," she answered brightly.

"And nothing else?" he pressed, frowning. "The look he was giving me seemed to say you came with the property."

"That's not the least bit true." Even if Luke chose to believe otherwise. After tonight, she couldn't deny that they shared a strong physical attraction, but that was nothing on which to base a life together. She didn't *love* Luke; how could she, when she was still in love with Clay? She'd been crazy about Clay Franklin most of her life, and feelings that intense wouldn't change overnight simply because he'd married another woman.

When Clay and Rorie announced their engagement, Kate had known with desolate certainty that she'd never love again. If she couldn't have Clay, then she would live the remainder of her life alone, treasuring the time they'd had together.

"You're sure Rivers has no claim on you?"

"None," Kate assured him.

"That's funny," Eric said with a humorless chuckle. "From the way he glared at me, I feel lucky to have walked away with my head still attached."

Kate forced a light laugh. "I'm sure you're mistaken."

Eric didn't comment further, but it was obvious he didn't believe her.

After their shaky beginning, dinner turned out to be an almost pleasant affair. Eric took Kate to the Red Bull, the one fancy restaurant in Nightingale, a steak house that specialized in thick T-bones and fat baked potatoes. A country-and-western band played local favorites in the lounge, which was a popular Friday-night attraction. The music drifted into the dining room, creating a festive atmosphere.

Eric studied the menu, then requested a bottle of wine with their meal.

When the waitress had taken their order, he planted his elbows on the table and smiled at Kate. "Your eyes are lovely," he said, his voice a little too enthusiastic.

Despite herself, Kate blushed. "Thank you."

"They're the same color as my ex-wife's." He announced this in bitter tones, as if he wished Kate's were any other color but blue. "I'm sorry," he added, looking chagrined. "I've got to stop thinking about Lonni. It's over. Finished. Kaput."

"I take it you didn't want the divorce."

"Do you mind if we don't talk about it?"

Kate felt foolish for bringing up the subject, especially since it was obviously so painful for him. "I'm sorry, that was thoughtless. Of course, you want to let go of the past."

The bottle of wine arrived and when Eric had sampled and approved it the waitress filled their glasses.

"Actually you remind me a good deal of Lonni," he said, after taking a sip of the chardonnay. "We met when we were both in college."

Kate lowered her gaze to her wineglass, twirling the delicate stem between her fingers. Eric was so clearly in love with his ex-wife that she wondered what had torn them apart.

"You were asking about the divorce?" He replenished his wine with a lavish hand.

"If it's painful, you don't need to talk about it."

"I don't think either Lonni or I ever intended to let matters go so far," he said, and Kate was sure he hadn't even heard her. "I certainly didn't, but before I knew what was happening the whole thing blew up in my face. There wasn't another man—I would have staked my life on that."

Their dinner salads arrived and, reaching for her fork, Kate asked, "What brought you to Nightingale?"

Eric drank his wine as though he were gulping cool water on a summer afternoon. "Lonni, of course."

"I beg your pardon?"

"Lonni. I decided I needed to make a clean break. Get a fresh start and all that."

"I see."

"You have to understand that when Lonni first suggested we might be better off separated, I thought it was the right thing to do. We hadn't been getting along and, frankly, if she wanted out of the relationship, I wasn't going to stand in her way. It's best to discover these things before children arrive, don't you agree?"

"Oh, yes." Kate nibbled at her salad, wondering what she could say that would help or comfort Eric.

An hour and another bottle of wine later, Kate realized he'd drunk the better part of both bottles and was in no condition to drive home. Now she had to tactfully make her date realize that.

"Do you dance?" she asked, as he paid the dinner bill.

He frowned slightly. "This country-and-western stuff doesn't usually appeal to me, but I'm willing to give it a whirl, if you are."

Kate supposed the wine he'd been drinking had quelled his reservations.

As she'd expected, the lounge was filled to capacity. Smoke and good humor filled the air, and when the band played a lively melody, Eric led Kate to the dance floor.

Kate was breathless by the time the song ended. To her relief, the next number was a much slower one. She realized her mistake the minute Eric locked her in his embrace. His hands fastened at the small of her back, forcing her close. She tried to put some space between them, but Eric didn't seem to notice her efforts. His eyes were shut as he swayed to the leisurely beat. Kate wasn't fooled; her newfound friend was pretending he had Lonni in his arms. It was a good thing her ego wasn't riding on this date.

"I need a little more room," she whispered.

He loosened his grip for a moment, but as the song continued his hold gradually tightened again. Kate edged her forearms up and braced them on his chest, easing herself back an inch or two.

"Excuse me, please." A harsh male voice that was all too familiar came from behind Eric. Kate wanted to crawl into a hole and die the instant she heard it.

"I'm cutting in," Luke informed the other man, who turned his head and looked at the intruder incredulously.

Without a word of protest Eric dropped his arms and took a step in retreat. Neither man bothered to ask Kate what *she* wanted. She was about to complain when Luke reached for her hand and with a natural flair swept her into his arms. The immediate sense of welcome she experienced made her want to weep with frustration.

"Why did you cut in like that?" she demanded. She felt disheartened and irritable. Everything she'd worked for this evening was about to be undone.

"Did you honestly mean for that city slicker to hold you so close?"

"How Eric holds me isn't any of your business."

"I'm making it my business."

His face was contorted with anger. His arms were so tight around her that Kate couldn't have escaped him if she'd tried. Judging by the looks they were receiving from the couples around them, Kate realized they were quickly becoming the main attraction.

The instant the music ended, Kate abruptly left Luke's arms and returned to Eric. Her date stood at the corner of the room, nursing a shot glass filled with amber liquid. Kate groaned and hid her displeasure. Eric had already had enough wine to drink without adding hard liquor.

"I thought you said there was nothing between you and Luke Rivers," he accused, when she joined him.

"There isn't. We're just good friends."

"That's not the impression I'm getting."

Kate didn't know how to respond. "I apologize for the interruption. Do you want to dance?"

"Not if it's going to cost me my neck."

"It isn't," she promised.

Another lively song erupted from the band. Eric reached for Kate's hand and she smiled encouragingly up at him. As they headed for the dance floor, Kate tried to ignore Luke's chilly glare.

Midway through the song, Eric stopped dancing. "I'm not into this fancy footwork," he declared. With that, he pulled her into his arms, tucking her securely against him.

"This is much better," he whispered, his mouth close to her ear. Once more his hold tightened.

"Eric, please. I'm having trouble breathing," Kate told him in a strangled voice.

"Oh, sorry." Immediately he relaxed his grip. "Lonni and I used to dance like this all the time."

Kate had already guessed as much. It was on the tip of her tongue to remind him that she wasn't his ex-wife, but she doubted it would make any difference.

Eric had spent much of the evening pretending she was.

At the moment, however, her date and his ex-wife were the least of Kate's problems. Tiny pinpricks moved up and down her spine, telling her that Luke was still glaring at her from the other side of the room. She did her best to act as though he wasn't there.

She smiled up at Eric; she laughed, she talked, but with each breath she drew, she could feel Luke's eyes on her, scrutinizing every move she made.

When the music ended, Eric returned to their table and his drink, swallowing the remainder of it in one gulp. The music started again and he pulled Kate toward him.

"I think I'll sit this one out." She hoped, that would appease Luke, who looked as if he were about to rip Eric in two. She'd never seen anyone look more furious. With the least bit of encouragement, his eyes told her, he'd cross the room and paddle her behind.

Her gaze dropped to her lap and she folded her hands, concentrating on not letting him know how much a single glance from him affected her.

"How much have you had to drink, Wilson?"

While her eyes were lowered, Luke had come over to their table. His voice was filled with angry demand.

"I can't say that it's any of your concern, Rivers." For his part, Eric seemed unnerved. He leaned back in his chair, balancing on two legs, and raised his empty shot glass.

"I don't agree," Luke countered, moving closer. "From what I can see, you've had plenty. I'm taking Kate home with me."

"Luke," she protested, "please don't do this."

"Your date's in no condition to drive."

It was all Kate could do not to stand up and defend Eric. Unfortunately Luke was right. She'd known it even before they'd finished dinner, but she wanted to handle things her own way.

"I can hold my liquor as well as the next man," Eric said, daring to wave his glass under Luke's nose. It was apparent to everyone that his courage had been fortified by whisky. Few men would have dared to taunt Luke in his present mood.

Luke turned to Kate. "You've got better sense than this, Kate."

Kate did have. But she had no intention of telling him so. "I think Eric knows his own limit," she returned.

"Then you plan to ride home with him?"

"I'm not sure yet." She wouldn't, but she wasn't about to hand Luke an armful of ammunition to use against her.

Luke scowled at her with such fury that it was difficult for Kate to swallow normally.

Slowly he turned to Eric. "If you value your teeth, I suggest you stay exactly where you are. Bob," Luke shouted to the sheriff's deputy across the room, "would you see this newcomer gets home without a problem?"

"Sure thing, Luke."

"Kate," he said, addressing her next, "you're coming with me."

"I most certainly am not."

Luke didn't leave her any option. He leaned forward and pulled her upright, as if she weighed no more than a bag of popcorn.

She struggled briefly, but she knew it was useless. "Luke, don't do this. Please, don't do this," she pleaded through clenched teeth, humiliated to the very roots of her hair.

"Either you come with me willingly or I carry you out of here." Luke's composure didn't falter. When she resisted, he swept his arms behind her legs and lifted her from the floor.

"Luke," Kate cried, "put me down this instant. I *demand* that you put me down."

He completely ignored her threat as he strode toward the door, his gaze focused impassively ahead of them. The waitress who had served her dinner came running up to hand Kate her coat and purse. Her eyes were flashing with humor.

"Stick by your man, honey," she advised. "That city slicker can't hold a candle to Luke Rivers."

"Luke's the man for you," someone else shouted. "When you two gonna tie the knot?"

Two men were holding open the lounge door for them. The last thing Kate heard as Luke carried her out into the cold night air was a robust round of applause from inside the lounge.

CHAPTER FIVE

"I HAVE NEVER BEEN so embarrassed in my life," Kate stormed as Luke parked his pickup outside the house. "How could you do that to me? How could you?"

During the entire ride home, Luke hadn't spoken a word, nor had he even glanced at her. He'd held himself stiff, staring straight ahead. For all his concern about her riding with Eric, he drove as if the very devil were on their tail. Only when they entered the long, winding driveway that led to the house had he reduced his speed.

"I'll never live this down," she told him, reaching for the door handle and vaulting out of the truck. She couldn't escape him fast enough. Every tongue in Nightingale would be wagging by morning, telling how Luke Rivers had hauled Kate Logan out of the Red Bull.

To her dismay Luke followed her into the house.

"I couldn't care less if you forgive me or not," he said darkly.

"The women were laughing and the men snickering.... I won't be able to show my face in this town again."

"As far as I'm concerned, that problem is one of your own making."

"That's not true!" She'd had no way of knowing that Eric was going to start downing wine like soda pop. The last thing she needed from Luke was a lecture. All she wanted him to do was leave, so she could lick her wounds in private and figure out how long it would be before she dared go out in public again.

Luke started pacing the kitchen floor. Each step was measured and precise. Clipped, like his voice.

"Please go," she beseeched wearily.

"I'm not leaving until I get some answers from you."

Gathering what remained of her dignity, which at this point wasn't much, Kate sank onto a chair. She wouldn't argue with Luke. Every time she tried, she came out the loser. Better to get this over with now rather than wait for tomorrow morning. She sighed deeply.

"Who the hell is Eric Wilson and why were you having dinner with him?" Luke demanded. His heavy boots clicked against the kitchen floor as he paced.

Instead of answering, Kate asked, "What's happened to us?" She gazed sorrowfully up at Luke. "Do you remember how much fun we used to have together? Tonight wasn't fun, Luke. Just a few weeks ago I could laugh with you and cry with you. You were my friend and I was yours. Suddenly nothing's the same, and I don't understand what's happened." Her voice wavered slightly. She fought an overwhelming desire to hide her face in her hands and weep.

She didn't win. Tears of pride and anguish spilled onto her cheeks. She brought her hands up, trying to hide her distress.

Luke knelt in front of her and pried her hands way. His fingers lightly and tenderly caressed her face. "Everything has changed, hasn't it, Princess?"

She sucked in a quavery breath and nodded.

"You're still confused, aren't you?" His hands cradled her face and he eased forward to press his warm mouth over hers. Even as she kissed him back, her confusion grew. He'd been so angry with her, more furious than she could ever remember. Yet, when he kissed her, he was achingly gentle.

Luke seemed to believe that her ready response to his kiss would answer the questions that haunted her. Instead it raised more reservations, more qualms.

"Do you understand now?" he asked, his voice a husky murmur, his eyes closed.

How Kate wished she did. She shook her head and lowered her gaze, bewildered and more uncertain than ever.

Luke stroked her lips with his index finger. His most innocent touches brought her nerves to life with a prickling, wary excitement. Not understanding her own impulse, she held his hand to her mouth and brushed her lips across his callused fingertips.

"Oh, love," he moaned, and bent forward, caressing her mouth with his once more. "We've got to put an end to this madness before I go insane."

"How?" she gasped, as she braced her hands against his broad chest. He felt so good, hard muscle and warm flesh, and so strong, as if nothing could stand in his way once he determined a course. Not heaven. Not hell. And nothing in between.

"How?" He repeated her question, then chuckled, the sound rumbling from deep from within his chest. "We're going to have to do as you suggested."

"What I suggested?"

His mouth continued to tease hers with a series of small, nibbling kisses that seemed almost to pluck at her soul. "There's only one way to cure what's between us, Kate, my love."

"One way," she echoed weakly.

"You'll have to marry me. There's no help for it and, frankly, the way I feel right now, the sooner the better."

Kate felt as if he'd dumped a bucket of ice water over her head. "Marry you," she cried, pushing him away with such force that he nearly toppled backward. "Your answer to all this confusion is for us to marry?"

"Kate, don't be unreasonable. We're perfect for each other. You need me now more than at any time in your life and I'm here for you."

"Luke, please—"

"No." He stopped her with one look. "You're about to lose everything in life that you thought was secure—your father and your home. I don't have any intention of taking over Devin's role, but the way I figure it, I'd make you a decent husband."

"What about love?" Kate cried.

Luke sighed in frustration. "We've gone over that ten times. You already love me—"

"Like a brother."

"Princess, sisters don't kiss their brothers the way you do me."

He apparently believed that was argument enough. Not knowing how else to respond, she shook her head. "I love Clay! You keep ignoring that or insisting I don't—but I do. I have for as long as I can remember. I can't marry you. I won't."

"For heaven's sake, forget Clay."

"It's not so easy!" she shouted.

"It would be if you'd try a little harder," Luke muttered, obviously losing patience. "I'm asking you to marry me, Kate Logan, and a smart woman like you should know a good offer when she hears one."

So much for love. So much for romance. Luke wasn't even listening to her, and Kate doubted he'd understood a single thing she'd said. "I don't think this conversation is getting us anywhere."

"Kate—"

"I think you should leave."

"Kate," he said, firmly gripping her shoulders, "how long is it going to take for you to realize that I love you and you love me?"

"Love you? How can you say that? Until a few weeks ago I was engaged to marry Clay Franklin!" Angrily she pushed away his hands and sprang to her feet.

"Yes. And all that time you were going to marry the wrong man."

Luke didn't seem to find that statement the least bit odd, as if women regularly chose to marry one man when they were really in love with another. Kate pushed her hair off her forehead and released a harsh breath.

"It's the truth," he said calmly.

She glared at him. Reasoning with Luke was a waste of time. He repeated the same nonsensical statements over and over, like a broken record, as if his few words were explanation enough.

"I'm going to bed," she said, turning abruptly away from him. "You can do as you like."

A moment of stunned silence followed her words before he chuckled softly, seductively. "I'm sure you don't mean that the way it sounds."

As KATE EXPECTED the small community buzzed with the news of her fiasco with Eric Wilson. Neighbor delighted in telling neighbor how Luke Rivers had swooped her into his arms and how the entire Friday-night crowd at the Red Bull had cheered as he'd carried her off the dance floor.

It took every ounce of courage Kate possessed just to walk down Main Street. Her smile felt stiff and false, like the painted smile on a china doll, and she was convinced she had the beginnings of an ulcer.

To worsen matters, all the townsfolk seemed to believe it was their place to offer her free advice.

"You stick with Luke Rivers. He's a far better man than that city slicker," the butcher told her Saturday afternoon.

Blushing heatedly, she ordered a pork roast and left as soon as she'd paid.

"I understand you and Luke Rivers caused quite a ruckus the other night at the steak house," the church secretary said Sunday morning after the service. "I heard about the romantic way Luke carried you outside."

Kate hadn't found being carried off the least bit romantic but she smiled kindly, made no comment and returned home without a word.

"What's this I hear about you and Luke Rivers?" The moment Kate entered her classroom Monday morning, Sally Daley appeared.

"Whatever you heard, I'm sure it was vastly exaggerated," Kate said hurriedly.

"That could be," Sally admitted with a delicate laugh. "You certainly know how to keep this town buzzing. First Clay's wedding reception, and now this.

By the way, Clay and Rorie are back from Hawaii, and I heard both of them have marvelous tans."

"That often happens in Hawaii," Kate said, sarcastically, swallowing the pain and holding on to her composure by the thinnest of threads.

No sooner had Sally left when Linda showed up. "Is it true?" she demanded, her eyes as round as quarters.

Kate shrugged. "Probably."

"Oh, good grief, the whole thing about squelching the rumors backfired, didn't it?"

Miserably Kate nodded. She feared she would dissolve into a puddle of tears the next time someone mentioned Luke's name. "After what happened to me Friday night, well . . . I just don't think it's possible to feel any more humiliated."

"I thought you said you hadn't met Eric," Linda said, clearly puzzled.

"I hadn't when you and I talked. Eric and I ran into each other at the grocery not ten minutes after you mentioned his name."

Linda slumped against the side of Kate's desk. "I try for months to meet a new man and nothing happens. It doesn't make sense. A few minutes after you decide you're looking, one pops up in front of you like a bird in a turkey shoot!"

"Beginner's luck." Except that Friday night could in no way be classified as lucky.

"Oh, Kate, you've really done it now."

"I know," she whispered in a tone of defeat.

Kate's day ended much as it had begun, which meant that by four o'clock she had a headache to rival all headaches. After school, she stopped in at the drugstore and bought a bottle of double-strength aspirin and some antacid tablets.

When she left the pharmacy, she headed for the library, wondering if Rorie would be back at work so soon following her honeymoon. Her friend's smiling face greeted Kate the instant she walked through the glass doors.

"Kate, it's so good to see you."

"Hi, Rorie." Kate still felt a little awkward with Clay's bride. She suffered no regrets about bringing them together, though it had been the most painful decision of her life.

"Sally Daley's right," Kate said with a light laugh, as she kissed Rorie's cheek. "You're so tanned. You look wonderful."

Rorie accept the praise with a lively smile that shone from her dark brown eyes. "To be honest, I never thought I'd get Clay to laze away seven whole days on the beach, but he did. Oh, Kate, we had the most wonderful time."

"I'm glad." And she was. Rorie and Clay belonged together—she'd known that almost from the beginning. Because of her sacrifice, their love had been given a chance. Rorie radiated happiness, and the glow of it warmed Kate's numb heart.

"I was just about to go on my coffee break. Have you got time to join me?" Rorie invited, glancing at her wristwatch.

"I'd love to." Kate crossed her fingers. With luck, Rorie wouldn't have heard any of the gossip—no doubt colorfully embroidered by now—about what had happened Friday night. At the moment, Kate needed a friend, a good friend, someone she could trust to be objective.

While Rorie arranged to leave the library in the hands of a volunteer assistant, Kate walked over to Nellie's Café, across the street from the pharmacy. She'd already ordered their coffee when Rorie slipped into the red upholstered booth across from her.

"Now what's this I've been hearing all day about you and Luke? Honestly, Kate, you know how to live dangerously, don't you? And now Luke's buying the Circle L and your father's marrying Mrs. Murphy. We were only gone seven days, but I swear it felt like a year with all Mary had to tell us once we got home."

Kate trained her expression to remain perfectly stoic, although the acid in her stomach seemed to be burning a hole straight through her. There were no secrets in this town.

"To tell you the truth, Luke and I haven't been getting along very well lately," she admitted, keeping her eyes lowered so as not to meet her friend's questioning gaze.

Rorie took a tentative sip of her coffee. "Do you want to talk about it?"

Kate nodded. She felt ridiculously close to tears and paid close attention to the silverware, repositioning the fork and the spoon several times as if their placement on the paper napkin were of dire importance.

"Luke was so gentle and good to me after you and Clay became engaged. He couldn't have been a better friend. Then . . . after the wedding I was feeling so lost and alone. Luke had been dancing with me and I felt so . . . secure in his arms, and I'm afraid I suggested something foolish . . . And now Luke keeps reminding me of it."

"That doesn't sound like Luke." Rorie frowned in puzzlement. "Nor does suggesting 'something foolish' sound like you."

"I had a glass of champagne on an empty stomach," Kate offered as an excuse.

"What about Luke?"

"I don't know, but I swear, he's become so unreasonable about everything, and he keeps insisting the most ridiculous things."

"Give me an example," Rorie said softly.

Kate shrugged. "He claims I love him."

Her remark was followed by a short silence. "What *do* you feel for Luke?" Rorie asked.

"I care about him, but certainly not in the way he assumes." Her finger idly circled the rim of the coffee cup while she composed her thoughts. "What irritates me most is that Luke discounts everything I felt for Clay, as if my love for him was nothing more than wasted emotion." Kate felt uncomfortable explaining this to her ex-fiancé's wife, but Rorie was the one person who would understand.

"And now that Clay's married to me," Rorie said, "Luke seems to think some giant light bulb has snapped on inside your brain."

"Exactly."

"He thinks you should have no qualms about throwing yourself into his loving arms?"

"Yes!" Rorie explained it far better than Kate had. "He keeps insisting I need him and that if I thought about it I'd realize I do love him. If it was only Luke I think I could deal with it, but everyone else in town, including my own father, thinks I should marry him."

"That's when you agreed to have dinner with that new attorney. What's his name again?"

"Eric Wilson. Yes, that was exactly the reason I went out with him. Rorie, I tell you I was desperate. Every time I turned around, Luke was there wearing this smug, knowing look and casually announcing that we'd be married before Christmas. He makes the whole thing sound like it's a foregone conclusion and if I resist him I'd be going against nature or something." She paused and dramatically waved her hand. "To hear Luke tell it, if I don't marry him by the end of the year, every herd in Nightingale is destined to deliver two-headed calves next spring."

Rorie laughed. "Is he really doing that?"

Kate nodded grimly. "Actually there's more." Although the truth was she had to tell Rorie everything. "To be fair you should know that I have no one to blame but myself. Luke may be doing all this talking about us getting married. But I was the one who... suggested it."

"How? When? Oh. The 'something foolish' you mentioned."

Shredding the paper napkin into tiny strips, Kate nodded again, swallowing painfully at the memory. "Honestly, Rorie, I didn't mean it. We were standing in the moonlight at your wedding dance and everything was so serene and beautiful. The words just slipped out of my mouth before I stopped to think what I was saying."

"The incident with the attorney didn't help."

Kate sighed. "And now that Dad's marrying Mrs. Murphy and Luke's bought the ranch everything's just getting worse."

"Luke can be a bit overpowering at times, can't he?"

Kate rolled her eyes in agreement.

"But you know, what bothers me even more than Luke's cavalier attitude is the way everyone else seems to be siding with him."

"What do you mean?"

"Look at my dad—he's the perfect example. As far as he's concerned, marrying Luke is only a matter of time. And everyone in town seems to think that since Clay married you, it's the only thing left for me to do. If I'm foolish enough to let another good man slip through my fingers, then I'll be sure to end up thirty and a spinster."

"That's ridiculous."

Coming from San Francisco, Rorie couldn't understand how differently people in this small Oregon community viewed life, Kate mused. A woman already thirty years old and unmarried was more than likely to stay that way—at least in Nightingale. "You haven't lived here long enough to understand how folks around here think."

"Kate, you're over twenty-one. No one can force you into marrying Luke. Remember that."

Kate rested her elbows on the table and cradled her coffee cup in both hands. "I feel caught in a current that's flowing much too fast for me. I don't dare stand up for fear I'll lose my footing but I can't just allow it to carry me where it will, either."

"No, you can't," Rorie said and her mouth tightened.

"Luke—and just about everyone else—apparently sees me as a poor, spineless soul who can't possibly decide what's best for her own life."

"That's not the least bit true," Rorie declared. "And don't let anyone tell you you're weak! If that were the case, you would have married Clay yourself instead of working so hard to make sure we found each other.''

Kate discounted that with a hard shake of her head. "I did the only thing I could.''

"But not everyone would have been so unselfish. Clay and I owe our happiness to you." She paused and gripped Kate's hands with her own. "I wish I knew how to help you. All I can tell you is to listen to your own heart.''

"Oh, Rorie, I feel so much better talking to you.'' Kate released a long, slow sigh, knowing her friend was right. She'd faltered for a step or two, but considering all that had happened to her in the past little while, that was understandable. Luke might believe she needed him, but she didn't, not really. In the weeks to come, she'd have the opportunity to prove it.

"Before I forget," Rorie said, her voice eager, "Clay and I want to invite you over for dinner one night soon. Like I said, we feel deeply indebted to you and want to thank you for what you did for us.''

"Dinner," Kate repeated, suddenly dismayed. She'd need time to fortify herself before facing Clay again. Here she was reassuring herself with one breath and then doubting herself in the next.

"Would next Tuesday be all right?'' Rorie pressed.

"But you've barely had time to settle in with Clay," Kate said, turning her attention back to her friend. "How about giving it another week or two?''

"Are you worried that I'm going to serve my special seafood fettuccine?'' Rorie asked with a light laugh. When she'd first found herself stranded in Nightingale, Rorie had cooked it for Clay and his younger brother, Skip, one night. But, unfortunately, because both men were involved in strenuous physical activity, they were far more interested in a hearty meat-and-potatoes meal at the end of the day. Neither of them had considered seafood swimming in a cream sauce and fancy noodles a very satisfactory repast, though Clay had politely tried to hide his disappointment. Skip hadn't.

Kate smiled at the memory of that night and slowly shook her head. "You serve whatever you want. I'm much easier to please than Skip."

"Actually Mary will probably do the cooking. She's been the Franklins' housekeeper for so many years that I don't dare invade her kitchen just yet. After the fettuccine disaster, she doesn't trust me around her stove any more than Skip does."

They both laughed, and to Kate, it felt good to forget her troubles, even for a few minutes.

"I should get back to library," Rorie announced reluctantly.

"I need to head home myself." Kate left some change on the table and slid out of the booth. Impulsively she hugged Rorie, grateful for the time they'd spent together and for the other woman's support. "I'm glad you're my friend," she whispered, feeling a little self-conscious.

"I am, too," Rorie said, and hugged her back.

By THE TIME Kate pulled into the Circle L driveway, she was filled with bold resolution. She hurried inside just long enough to set a roast in the oven and change her clothes. Then, she went into the yard, intent on confronting Luke. The sooner she talked to him, the better she'd feel.

As luck would have it, Luke wasn't in any of the places where she normally found him. Bill Schmidt, a longtime ranch hand, was working in the barn by himself.

"Bill, have you seen Luke around?" she asked.

Bill straightened slowly and set his hat farther back on his head. "Can't say I have. At least, not in the past couple of hours. The last thing he said was he was going out to look for strays. I imagine he'll be back pretty soon now."

"I see." Kate gnawed her lower lip, wondering what she should do. Without pausing to question the wisdom of her decision, she reached for a bridle.

"Bill, would you get Nonstop for me?" Nonstop was the fastest horse in their stable. Kate was in the mood for some exercise; if she didn't find Luke, that was fine, too. She could use a good hard ride to vent some of the frustration that had been binding her all week.

"Sure, Mizz Logan." Bill left his task and headed for the corral, returning a few minutes later with Nonstop. "Luke seemed to be in the mood to do some riding himself this afternoon," he commented as he helped her cinch the saddle. "Must be something in the air."

"Must be," Kate agreed.

Minutes later Nonstop was cantering out of the yard. Kate hadn't ridden in several weeks and she was surprised to realize just how long it had been. When she was engaged to Clay, she'd spent many a summer afternoon in the saddle, many a Saturday or Sunday riding by his side. That had ended about the same time as their wedding plans. She felt a stinging sense of loss but managed to dispel it with the memory of her talk with Rorie earlier.

Bill pointed out the general direction Luke had taken, and Kate followed that course, at a gallop. She found it wonderfully invigorating to be in the saddle again.

The afternoon remained mild, but the breeze carried the distinctive scent of autumn. These past few days had been Indian summer, with rare clement temperatures. Within the hour, the sun would set, bathing the rolling green hills in a golden haze.

"Kate." Her name floated on a whisper of wind.

Pulling back on the reins, Kate halted the mare and twisted around to discover Luke trotting toward her. She raised her hand and waved. Much of her irritation had dissipated, replaced by a newly awakened sense of well-being. No longer did Kate feel her life was roaring out of control; she was in charge, and it exhilarated her.

Luke leapt out of the saddle as soon as he reached her. "Is everything all right?"

"Of course," she said, laughing a little. "I hope I didn't frighten you?"

"No. I rode into the yard not more than fifteen minutes after you left, according to Bill. I was afraid I wasn't going to catch you. You were riding like a demon."

"I . . . had some thinking to do."

"Bill said you were looking for me."

"Yes," she agreed. "I wanted to talk to you." There was no better time than the present. And no better place. They were at the top of a grassy knoll that looked out over the lush green valley below. Several head of cattle dotted the pasture spread out below them, lazily grazing in the last of the afternoon sun.

Luke lifted his hand to her waist, helping her out of the saddle. His eyes held hers as he slowly lowered her to the ground. Once again, she was aware that his touch had a curious effect on her, but she stringently ignored it.

Still, Kate's knees felt a little shaky and she was more breathless than she should have been after her ride. She watched Luke loop the reins over the horses heads to dangle on the ground. Both Nonstop and Silver Shadow, Luke's gelding, were content to graze leisurely.

"It's lovely out this afternoon, isn't it?" she said, then sank down on the grass and drew up her legs, resting on her knees.

Luke sat down beside her, looking out over the valley. "It's a rare day. I don't expect many more like it."

"Rorie and Clay are back from Hawaii."

Luke had removed his leather work gloves to brush a stray curl from her temple, then stopped abruptly and withdrew his hand. "I take it you saw Rorie?"

She nodded, adding, "We had coffee at Nellie's."

"You're not upset?"

"Not at all."

"I thought you looked more at peace with yourself." He leaned back and rested his weight on the palms of his hands. His long legs were stretched out in front of him, crossed at the ankles. "Did you finally recognize that you never did love Clay? That you're in love with me?"

"No," she said vehemently, amazed he could anger her so quickly.

Luke turned away. "I thought...I'd hoped you were willing to discuss a wedding date," he said stiffly.

"Oh, Luke," she whispered and closed her eyes. He was so worried for her, so concerned, and it really wasn't necessary. And she didn't know how to reassure him.

"Luke," she said softly, "we've been having the same discussion all week, and it's got to come to an end." Luke faced her and their eyes met with an impact that shocked her. "Luke, I think you're a wonderful man—I have for years and years," she continued quickly. "But I don't love you, at least not the way you deserve to be loved."

Luke's eyebrows soared, then his brow furrowed. He seemed about to argue, but Kate stopped him before he had the chance.

"I refuse to be coerced into a wedding simply because *you* feel it's the best thing for me—because you feel I need looking after. Frankly, I don't believe marriage is a good idea for us—at least not to each other."

"Kate, love—"

Lowering her lashes in an effort to disguise her frustration, Kate reminded him for what seemed the thousandth time, "I am not your 'love.'"

His eyes became sharp, more intent. "Then explain," he said slowly, "why it feels so right when I hold you? How do you answer that?"

She avoided his gaze, her eyes focusing a fraction below his own, resting instead on the slight cleft in his chin. "I can't explain it any more than I can deny it." She'd willingly give him that much. "I do enjoy it when you kiss me, though I don't know why, especially since I'm still in love with Clay. My guess is that we've lived all these years in close proximity and we're such good friends that it was a natural, comforting, thing to do. But I don't think it should continue."

His nostrils flared briefly, and from the impatient look he gave her, she could tell he was angered by her words.

"I'm asking you, Luke, pleading with you, if you—"

"Kate, would you listen to me for once?"

"No," she said firmly, holding her ground. "I want only one thing from you, and that's for you to drop this incessant pressure that we marry."

"But—"

"I want your word, Luke."

His entire countenance changed, and just looking at him told Kate how difficult he was finding this. "All right," he said heavily. "You have my word. I won't mention it again."

Kate sighed shakily and all her muscles seemed to go limp. "Thank you," she whispered. "That's all I want."

Luke lunged to his feet and reached for Silver Shadow's reins. He eased himself back into the saddle, then paused to gaze down at her, his face dark and brooding. "What about what I want, Kate? Did you stop to consider that?"

CHAPTER SIX

KATE FELT GOOD. The lethargy and depression she'd been feeling since Clay's wedding had started to dissipate. She'd completely adjusted to the idea of her father's impending marriage. And even the sale of the Circle L—to Luke of all people—no longer seemed so devastating. Clearing the air between them had helped, too.

"Evening, Nellie," Kate called as she entered the small, homey café. She'd arrived home from school to discover a message from her father suggesting she meet him for dinner at Nellie's at six sharp.

"Howdy, Kate," Nellie called from behind the counter.

Kate assumed her father would be bringing Dorothea so they could discuss last-minute plans for their wedding, which was scheduled for Friday evening at the parsonage. Minnie Wilkins, Pastor Wilkins's wife, and Dorothea were close friends. Kate was to stand up for Dorothea and Luke for her father in the small, private ceremony.

Carrying the water glass in one hand, a coffeepot in the other and a menu tucked under her arm, Nellie followed Kate to the booth. "I'm expecting my dad and Dorothea Murphy to join me," Kate explained.

"Sure thing," Nellie said. "The special tonight is Yankee pot roast, and when your daddy gets here, you tell him I pulled a rhubarb pie out of the oven no more than fifteen minutes ago.''

"I'll tell him."

"Nellie, I could use a refill on my coffee," Fred Garner called from the table closest to the window. He nodded politely in Kate's direction. "Good to see you again, Kate."

"You, too, Fred." She smiled at the owner of Garner Feed and Supply and noted that a couple of ranchers were dining with him. Glancing at her watch, Kate realized her father was a few minutes late, which wasn't like him.

To pass the time she began reading the menu; she was halfway through when the door opened. Smiling automatically, she glanced up and discovered Luke striding toward her. He slid into her booth, opposite her.

"Where's your dad?"

"I don't know. He asked me to meet him here for dinner."

"I got the same message."

"I think it's got something to do with the wedding."

"No," Luke muttered, frowning. "I've got some bank forms he needs to sign."

Nellie brought another glass of water, then poured coffee for both of them.

"Evening, Nellie."

"Luke Rivers, I declare I don't see near enough of you," the older woman said coyly, giving him a bold wink as she sauntered away with a swish of her hips.

Astonished that Nellie would flirt so openly with Luke, Kate took a sip of her coffee and nearly scalded her tongue. Why, Nellie had a good fifteen years on Luke!

"Does she do that often?" Kate asked, in a disapproving whisper.

"You jealous?"

"Of course not. It's just that I've never known Nellie to flirt quite so blatantly."

"She's allowed." Luke gazed down at his menu and to all appearances, was soon deep in concentration.

Kate managed to squelch the argument before it reached her lips. There wasn't a single, solitary reason for her to care if a thousand women wanted to throw themselves at Luke Rivers. She had no claim on him, and wanted none.

The restaurant telephone pealed, but with four plates balanced on her arms, Nellie let it ring until someone in the kitchen answered it.

No more than a minute later, she approached their table. "That was Devin on the phone. He says he's going to be late and you two should go ahead and order." She pulled a notepad from the pocket of her pink uniform. "Eat hearty since it's on his tab," she said, chuckling amiably.

"The roast-beef sandwich sounds good to me," Kate said. "With a small salad."

"I'll have chicken-fried steak, just so I can taste those biscuits of yours," Luke told the café owner, handing her the menu. "I'll start with a salad, though."

"I got rhubarb pie hot from the oven."

"Give me a piece of that, too," Luke said, grinning up at Nellie.

"Kate?"

"Sure," she said, forcing a smile. "Why not?"

Once Nellie had left, an awkwardness fell between Kate and Luke. To Kate if felt as though they'd become strangers with each other, standing on uncertain ground.

Luke ventured into conversation first. "So how's school?"

"Good. Really good."

"That's nice."

She laughed nervously. "I've started washing down cupboards at the house, clearing out things. I've got two piles. What Dad's going to take with him and what I'll need when I move."

Instead of pleasing Luke, her announcement had the opposite effect. "You're welcome to live on the ranch as long as you want," he said, his dark eyes narrowing. "There's no need to move away."

"I know that, but the Circle L belongs to you—or it will soon."

"It's your home."

"It won't be much longer," she felt obliged to remind him. "I'm hoping to find a place in town. In fact, I'm looking forward to the move. You know what the roads are like in the winter. I should have done this long ago."

"You wouldn't have to move if you weren't so damn stubborn," Luke muttered between clenched teeth, clearly struggling with his patience. "I swear, Kate, you exasperate me. The last thing I want to do is take your home away from you."

"I know that." She hadn't considered relocating to town earlier for a number of reasons, foremost being that her father had needed her. But he didn't anymore, and it was time for her to exhibit a little independence.

Nellie delivered their tossed green dinner salads, lingering at the table to flirt with Luke again. He waited until she'd left before he leaned forward, speaking to Kate in a low, urgent voice. His mouth was tight and his eyes were filled with regret. "Kate, please stay on at the ranch. Let me at least do this much for you."

She thanked him for his concern with a warm smile, but couldn't resist adding, "People will talk." After all Luke had pointed that very fact out to her when she'd made her foolish proposal. The night of Clay's wedding...

"Let them talk."

"I'm a schoolteacher, remember?" she whispered. She felt genuinely grateful for his friendship and wanted to assure him that all this worry on her behalf wasn't necessary, that she was fully capable of living on her own.

Their dinner arrived before they'd even finished the salads. Another silence fell over them as they ate. Several possible subjects of conversation fluttered in and out of Kate's mind as the meal progressed. Her fear was that Luke would divert the discussion back to the ranch no matter what she said, so she remained silent.

A sudden commotion came from the sidewalk outside the café.

"It's Harry Ackerman again," Fred Garner shouted to Nellie, who was busy in the kitchen. "You want me to call the sheriff?"

"No, let him sing," Nellie shouted back. "He isn't hurting anyone."

Harry Ackerman was the town drunk. Back in his and Nellie's high-school days, they'd dated seriously, but then Harry went into the military and returned to Nightingale more interested in the bottle than a wife and family. Within six months, Nellie had married a mechanic who'd drifted into town. Problem was, when he left, he didn't take Nellie or their two children with him. But Nellie hadn't seemed to miss him much, and had supported her family by opening the café, which did a healthy business right from the first.

Fifteen years had passed, and Harry was still courting Nellie. Every time he came into town, he took it upon himself to sing love songs from the sidewalk outside the café. He seemed to believe that would be enough of an inducement for her to forget the past and finally marry him.

"Actually his singing voice isn't so bad," Kate murmured to Luke.

Luke chuckled. "I've heard better."

Fred Garner stood up and strolled toward the cash register. He glanced in Luke's direction and touched the rim of his hat in greeting. "I've been hearing things about the two of you," Fred said, grinning broadly.

Kate centered her concentration on the sandwich, refusing to look up from her plate.

Luke made a reply that had to do with the ranch and not Kate, and she was grateful.

"Be seeing you," Fred said as he headed toward the door. As he opened it, Harry's latest love ballad, sung badly off-key, could be heard with ear-piercing clarity.

Fred left and soon Harry Ackerman strolled inside. He glanced longingly at Nellie, placed his hand over his heart and started singing again at the top of his lungs.

"You get out of my restaurant," Nellie cried, reaching for the broom. "I don't want you in here disrupting my customers." She wielded the broom like a shotgun, and before she could say another word Harry stumbled outside. He pressed his forlorn face to the glass, content to wait until his one true love returned to his waiting arms.

"Sorry, folks," Nellie muttered, replacing the broom.

"No problem," Luke answered, and she tossed him a grateful smile, then hurried over to refill their coffee cups.

The disturbance died down when Harry wandered down the street to find a more appreciative audience. Luke sighed as he stirred his coffee slowly and carefully. "I don't think your father has any intention of showing up tonight," he began. "In fact—"

"Why, that's ridiculous," Kate said, cutting him off. "Dad wouldn't do that."

"He's trying to tell you something," Luke insisted.

"I can't imagine what." She could, but decided to pretend otherwise.

For a long moment, Luke said nothing. "You're smart enough to figure it out, Kate." He finished off the last bite of his pie and pushed the plate aside. "I've got some things to attend to, so I'd best be leaving." The crow's feet at the corners of his eyes crinkled with amusement as he glanced out the café window. "Who knows, you might be singing me love songs in a couple of years if you don't come to your senses soon."

Kate ignored the comment. "My father will be here any minute."

"No, Princess," Luke said, and the smile drained from his dark eyes. He leaned across the table to brush his hand gently against her cheek. "But his message is coming across loud and clear."

Kate stayed at the café another half hour after Luke had left and it took her that long to admit he was right. Her father *had* been giving her a message, this one no more subtle than the rest. Expelling her breath in disgust, Kate dredged up a smile and said goodbye to Nellie.

KATE DIDN'T SEE Luke again until Friday evening, when they met at the Wilkins' home for her father's wedding. Kate arrived with Devin, and Luke followed a few minutes later. Kate was busy arranging freshly baked cookies on a tray for the small reception to be held after the ceremony, when Luke walked into the dining room. Dorothea was with Minnie Wilkins in the back bedroom, and her father and Pastor Wilkins were talking in the living room.

"Hello, Kate," Luke said from behind her.

"Hi," she responded, turning to give him a polite smile. Her breath stopped in her throat at the elegant yet virile sight he made. He was dressed in a dark, three-piece suit that did nothing to disguise his strong, well formed body, and his light blue silk tie enhanced the richness of his tan. Kate suspected that Luke was basking in the wonder she was unable to conceal, and yet still she couldn't stop looking at him.

Her heart skipped a beat, then leapt wildly as his penetrating brown eyes looked straight into hers. She felt the tears well up, knowing that only Luke truly understood how difficult this evening was for her.

Many of her emotions tonight were identical to the ones she'd experienced at Clay's and Rorie's wedding. All day, she'd worried her stomach into a knot of apprehension. The acceptance and strength of purpose she'd so recently been feeling had fled. Tonight, she was reminded again that everything she loved, everything familiar, had been taken from her life. First the man she'd planned to marry, now her father, and soon, so very soon, her childhood home. It was too much change, too quickly.

Just as she had at Clay's wedding, Kate forced herself to show pleasure, to behave appropriately. She *was* happy for her father and Dorothea—just as she'd been for Clay and Rorie. But why did everyone else's happiness need to cost Kate so much?

Luke must have read the apprehension in her eyes, because he hurried to her side. "Everything's going to be all right," he told her quietly.

"Of course it is," she said, braving a smile. She turned back to the flowers, although her fingers were trembling. "I couldn't have chosen a better wife for Dad myself. Dorothea's wonderful."

Luke's hands settled on her shoulders and began to caress them gently. "So are you, Princess."

It demanded every ounce of fortitude Kate possessed not to whirl around and bury her face in Luke's chest, to absorb his strength. But this was exactly how she'd lost control before; she had to remember that.

A sound came from behind them, and Luke released her with a reluctance that echoed her own. She needed Luke now, just as she'd needed him a few weeks before. But this time, she was determined to be stronger.

The ceremony itself was brief. Kate felt almost wooden as she stood next to the woman her father had chosen to replace her mother. Memories of the lovely, soft-spoken Nora, and of their happy, close-knit family, almost overwhelmed Kate. Twice she felt tears threaten, but managed to hold them in. Both times she found Luke's eyes on her, his gaze warm with empathy.

When Pastor Wilkins closed his Bible and announced that Devin and Dorothea were now husband and wife, Devin took his bride in his arms and gently kissed her. Minnie Wilkins dabbed at her eyes with a lace hankie.

"You look so lovely," the woman murmured, hugging her friend.

Soon they were all hugging each other. When Kate's arms slipped around Luke it felt like a homecoming. It felt far too comfortable, too familiar, and that frightened her. She stiffened and let her arms drop. Luke would have none of that, however. Locking his hands on her upper arms he drew her back to him.

"What I wouldn't give for a full moon and some champagne," he whispered in her ear.

Kate could have done without his teasing, but she refused to satisfy him with a reply.

The small reception began immediately afterward, and Kate was busy for the next hour, dishing up pieces of wedding cake, passing trays of sugar cookies and pouring coffee.

Her father found her in the kitchen, his eyes bright with happiness. "You're going to be just fine, aren't you, Princess?"

"You know I am," she said, flashing him a brilliant smile.

"Dorothea and I will be leaving soon." He placed his arm around her shoulder and hugged her. "Don't forget I love you. You'll always be my little girl."

"You'll always be my hero."

Devin chuckled. "I think Luke would like to fill that position and I'd be more than pleased if he did. He's a good man, sweetheart. You could do a lot worse."

"Dad," she groaned, closing her eyes. "Luke is wonderful, and I understand your concern. You'd like all the loose ends neatly tied up before you leave for your honeymoon, but I'm just not ready to make a commitment. At least not yet."

"You'd make a lovely country bride, Princess. I just want you to be happy."

"I will be," she said, standing on the tips of her toes to kiss his cheek.

By the time Devin and Dorothea were ready to leave, more than twenty close friends had gathered at the parsonage. They crowded onto the porch to send the newlyweds off with a flourish of kisses and enthusiastic waves. Almost everyone returned to the warmth of the house but Kate lingered, not wanting to go back inside when tears were blurring her eyes.

Luke joined her, standing silently at her side until she'd composed herself.

"Your father asked me to see you home."

Kate nodded and swallowed a near-hysterical laugh. Despite their conversation Devin was still attempting to throw her together with Luke.

"You mean you aren't going to argue with me?" Luke asked with exaggerated surprise.

"Would it do any good?"

"No," he said and chuckled lightly. Then, suddenly, his strong arms encircled her stiff body. "It's been a long time since you let me kiss you," he said, his warm breath closer and closer to her mouth.

Kate stared at his chest, refusing to raise her eyes to his. Gathering her resolve, she snapped her head up to demand he release her. But Luke smothered her words with his mouth. Her hands closed into tight fists as soon as the initial shock had subsided and she fully intended to push him away. But once his mouth had settled over hers, he gentled the kiss, and her resolve all but disappeared.

Again and again his mouth sought hers. Luke's sweet, soft kisses seemed to erase all the pain from her heart. Only a moment before, she'd been intent on escaping. Now she clung to him, tilting her face toward him, seeking more. He deepened his kiss, sending jolts of excitement through her.

His hands were in her hair, holding her prisoner as he devoured her. When he stopped abruptly, Kate moaned her dissatisfaction.

"Kate..." he warned.

"Hmm...Luke, don't stop."

"I'm afraid we've attracted an audience," he returned mildly.

Sucking in her breath, Kate dropped her arms and whirled around so fast she would have stumbled if Luke's arms hadn't caught her. Her eyes felt as wide as the Columbia River as she stared into the faces of the twenty or more guests who'd stepped outside, preparing to leave.

"I THOUGHT Taylor Morgenroth should play the part of the Indian chief," Kate was saying to Linda when Sally Daley walked into the faculty lounge Monday afternoon. The two were discussing the final plans for their Thanksgiving play.

"Taylor's the perfect choice," Linda agreed.

"I see you girls are busy," Sally commented. "This play is such an ambitious project. You two are to be commended."

"Thanks." Linda answered for them both, trying to ignore the other woman as much as possible.

"Wasn't that Rorie Franklin I saw you with the other day, Kate, dear?"

"Yes. We had coffee together at Nellie's." She resumed her discussion with Linda, not wanting to be rude to Sally, but at the same time, hoping to dissuade her from further conversation.

But Sally refused to be thwarted. She settled in the chair opposite Kate, and said in confidential tones, "You're completely recovered from Clay Franklin now, aren't you, dear?"

Kate shared an exasperated look with Linda and nearly laughed out loud when the third-grade teacher playfully rolled her eyes toward the ceiling. To hear Sally talk, anybody would think Kate had recently recovered from a bad case of the flu.

"Sally, honestly!" Kate exclaimed when she realized how avidly the other woman was waiting for her reply. "How am I supposed to answer that?" She dramatically covered her heart with one hand and offered a look meant to portray misery and anguish. "Do you want me to tell you that my female pride's been shattered and that I'll never love again?"

Sally shook her head. "I wouldn't believe it, anyway."

"Then why ask?" Linda prompted.

"Well, because we all love Kate. She's such a dear, and she's been through so much lately."

"Thank you," Kate said graciously, then returned her attention to the Thanksgiving project.

"Most of the fuss about you and Eric Wilson and Luke Rivers has died down now," Sally assured her, as if this should lessen the keen embarrassment of that Friday night.

"I take it you haven't talked to Eric lately?" Linda asked, surprising Kate with her sudden interest. There'd been plenty of opportunity to inquire about the attorney, but Linda hadn't done so until now.

"Talked to him?" Kate echoed with a short, derisive laugh. "I don't even shop at the Safeway store for fear I'll run into him again."

"I don't think you need to worry," Sally said blandly. "From what I understand, he's avoiding you, too."

Linda snickered softly. "No doubt. I'm sure Luke Rivers put quite a scare into him."

"How do you mean?" Kate demanded, already angry with Luke.

"You don't know?" Sally asked, her eyes sparkling with excitement.

"Know what?" Kate swung her gaze first to Linda, then to Sally. "Did Luke threaten him?" If he had, he was going to hear about it from her.

"I haven't got the foggiest idea what Sally's talking about," Linda said quickly.

"I didn't hear anything specific," Sally confirmed sheepishly. "I thought maybe you had . . ." The older teacher's expression suggested that she hoped Kate would fill in the succulent details herself. "My dear, surely you understand that everyone in town is speculating about you and Luke," she continued.

"Rumors have been floating around since the day of Clay's wedding," Linda added.

"But Sally just finished telling me those were dying down," Kate snapped, irritated with the entire discussion.

"They're not about you and that Wilson fellow," Sally rushed to explain. "As far as your one date with him is concerned, it's history. He's too smart to cross Luke."

"I'm sure he is," Kate said, anxious to quell the woman's gossip. "Aren't we about finished here, Linda?" she asked pointedly.

"Ah ... yes."

"Now folks are talking about seeing you and Luke together at Nellie's last week just before your father's wedding, and there've been a few rumors flying around about seeing the two of you at Pastor Wilkins's, too."

As fast as her hands would cooperate, Kate started gathering up their materials. Sally seemed to accept that she was about to lose her audience. If she'd come to pump Kate for information she'd just have to realize Kate wasn't talking. Standing, Sally gave a deep sigh, clearly disappointed. She reached for her purse and headed out the door, pausing to look back. "Frankly, I think Fred Garner is carrying this thing between you and Luke just a little too far. I consider what he's doing in poor taste." With that, she left the room.

"Fred Garner?" Linda echoed after a stunned second. "What's that old coot doing now?"

"Fred Garner owns the feed store," Kate said, wondering what Sally could possibly mean.

"Yes, but what's he got to do with anything?"

"Beats me." Still, Kate couldn't help wondering. Fred had seen them at the restaurant, and he'd been at the reception for her father and Dorothea. Although she hadn't seen him on the porch when a number of guests had found her in Luke's arms, she had very little doubt that he was there.

When Kate drove home an hour later, Luke was working in the yard. She climbed out of the car, took two steps toward him and halted abruptly. The lump in her throat was so large she could hardly swallow, let alone speak.

The trembling had started the minute she left Garner Feed and Supply. She'd dropped in at the store following Sally's puzzling remark, and from then on everything had grown progressively worse. The way she felt right now, she could slam her purse over Luke's head, or something equally violent, and feel completely justified.

"Kate?" he asked gently, looking concerned. "What's wrong?"

She knew her feelings were written on her face. Her heart felt like a piston from a fired-up jalopy. She'd never been more scandalized in her life, which was saying a great deal considering the fiasco with Eric Wilson.

In fact, the blow her dignity had been dealt by Luke Rivers during that incident paled by comparison with this latest outrage. Dear Lord, there was only one thing for her to do. She'd have to move away from Nightingale.

"This is all your doing, isn't it?" she demanded in a shaking voice. She held her head high, although it was a struggle to preserve her composure. Her pride was all she had left, and that was crumbling at her feet.

Luke advanced several steps toward her. "What are you talking about?"

She ground her fist into her hip. "I just got back from the feed store. Does that tell you anything?"

"No."

"I'll just bet."

He frowned. "Kate, I swear to you, I don't know what you're talking about."

She made a doubting noise that came out sounding and feeling like a painful sob. Yet he appeared so bewildered. She didn't know how any man could cause her such life-shattering embarrassment and maintain that look of faithful integrity.

The tears wouldn't be restrained any longer, and they slipped from her eyes, running down the sides of her face. They felt cool against her flushed cheeks.

"Kate? What's wrong?"

Kate turned and rapidly walked away from him rather than allow him to witness her loss of control. She hurried into the house and slumped in a chair, hiding her face in her hands as she battled the terrible urge to weep hysterically. The painful sensation in the pit of her stomach grew more intense every time she drew a breath.

The door opened and she said, "Go away."

"Kate?"

"Haven't . . . you . . . done . . . enough?" Each word rolled from her tongue on the end of a hiccuping sob.

He knelt in front of her and wrapped his arms around her, holding her close, but she pushed him away, refusing the comfort he offered.

Kate's shoulders still heaved. With an exasperated sigh, Luke stood back on his boot heels and buried his hands in his pockets. "All right, tell me about it."

"Pastor ... Wilkins ... bet ... twenty ... dollars ... on ... December," she told him between sobs. Her fingers curled into fists. "Even...Clay...put in a...wager."

Seeing his name on that huge blackboard had hurt more than anything.

"Kate, I swear to you by everything I hold dear that I don't know what you're talking about."

Furiously she wiped the tears from her face and tried to marshal her composure enough to speak clearly. "The...feed store," she managed.

"What about the feed store?"

"They're taking bets—it's a regular lottery," she cried, all the more furious with him because he was making her spell out this latest humiliation.

"Bets on what?" Luke's frown was growing darker by the second, and Kate could tell that he was dangerously close to losing his patience.

"On us!" she cried, as if that much, at least, should be obvious.

"For what?"

"When we're going to be married!" she shouted. "What else? Half the town's got money riding on the date of our wedding."

"Dear Lord," Luke moaned, briefly closing his eyes, as if he couldn't quite believe what she was telling him.

"You honestly didn't know?"

"Of course not." He was beginning to look perturbed as only Luke could. His dark eyes took on a cold glare that was enough to intimidate the strongest of men. "How'd you find out?"

"Sally Daley said something about it after school, and then in the school parking lot one of the mothers told me March is a lovely time of year for a wedding. March sixteenth, she said. Then...then I made the mistake of stopping in at the feed store on my way home to check out what was going on."

Luke nodded, but Kate had the impression he was only half listening to her.

"As far as I'm concerned, there's only one thing for me to do," she said, gaining strength from her decision. "I'll offer my resignation to the school board tomorrow morning and leave the district this weekend."

Luke flashed her a quick, angry look. "That won't be necessary. I'll take care of this my own way."

CHAPTER SEVEN

AT ONE TIME Kate spent as many hours at Elk Run, the Franklin stud farm, as she did at the Circle L. But when she arrived Tuesday night for dinner, Elk Run no longer felt familiar. It seemed like years instead of weeks since her last visit. Kate's enthusiasm for this dinner with Clay and Rorie had never been high, but now she felt decidedly uncomfortable.

"Kate, welcome." Rorie flew out the door the minute Kate pulled into the driveway. She stepped from the car into Rorie's hug.

Clay Franklin followed his wife and briefly held Kate close, smiling down on her the same way he always had from the time she was thirteen. Back then, she'd worshiped him from afar, and she'd worshiped him more with each passing year. Kate paused, waiting for the surge of regret and pain she'd been expecting; to her astonishment, it didn't come.

"We're so pleased you could make it," Rorie said as she opened the door for her.

Recognizing Kate, Clay's old dog, Blue, ambled over for his usual pat. Kate was more than happy to comply and bent down to playfully scratch his ears.

Mary, the Franklins' housekeeper, bustled about the kitchen, dressed in her bib apron, hair twisted into thick braids and piled on top of her head. Kate could scarcely remember a time she hadn't seen Mary in an apron. The scent of freshly baked pie permeated the room, mingling with the hearty aroma of roast beef and simmering vegetables.

"I hope that's one of your award-winning pies I'm smelling, Mary," Kate coaxed. "I've had my heart set on a thick slice all day."

"Oh, get away with you," Mary returned gruffly, but the happy light that sparked from her eyes told Kate how gratified the housekeeper was by her request.

"When are you going to give me your recipe?" Kate asked, although she didn't know whom she'd be baking pies for now that her father had remarried. "No one can bake an apple pie the way you do."

"Mary won't even share her secret with me," Rorie said, giving a soft laugh. "I don't think she's willing to trust a city slicker just yet."

"I never wrote down any recipe," Mary grumbled, casting Rorie a stern look. "I just make my pies the same way everybody else does."

"I wish I could bake like Mary does," Rorie said, slipping her arm around her husband's waist. They exchanged a meaningful glance. The way Clay smiled at his wife showed he couldn't care less whether or not she could bake a pie.

Once more Kate braced herself for the pain of seeing them together, gentle and loving, but to her surprise she didn't feel so much as a pinprick of distress. She relaxed, wondering at what was happening, or rather wasn't, and why.

"Where's Skip?" she asked suddenly. She missed Clay's younger brother almost as much as she did Clay. The two had been friends for years.

"Football practice," Clay explained. "He's quarterback this year and proud as a peacock about it. He'll be home later."

"About the time Mary serves her pie," Rorie whispered to Kate. Skip's appetite for sweets was legendary.

The small party headed into the homey living room. The piano rested against one wall, and Kate noted the music on the stand. It had always been Kate who'd played that piano, but Rorie played for Clay now. There had been a time when Kate and Clay had sung together, their voices blending in a melodious harmony. But Clay sang with Rorie now.

Kate expected the knowledge to claw at her insides, and she did feel a small twinge of regret—but that was all.

"Skip's hoping to catch you later," Rorie explained.

"As I recall, you played quarterback your senior year of high school," Kate reminded Clay as she claimed the overstuffed chair. "That was the first year the Nightingale team made it to the state finals."

Rorie beamed a look of surprise at her husband. "You never told me that."

"There wasn't much to tell," Clay said with a short laugh. "We were eliminated in the first round." He sat beside Rorie and draped his arm around her shoulders as if he had to keep touching her to believe she was here at his side.

Mary carried in a tray of wineglasses and an unopened bottle of a locally produced sparkling white. "I take it Devin and Dorothea arrived safely in California?" she asked as she uncorked the wine.

"Yes, Dad phoned when they arrived at Dorothea's daughter's house."

"We didn't get a chance to say more than a few words at the reception," Rorie apologized. "You were so busy pouring coffee, there wasn't much opportunity to chat."

"I know. It was good of you and Clay to come."

"We wouldn't have missed it for the world," Clay said.

"I wanted to tell you how nice your father and Dorothea looked together. And for that matter, you and Luke, too," Rorie added.

"Thank you," Kate said simply, wondering if her friends had heard about the incident on the Wilkins's front porch. It still embarrassed Kate to think of all her father's friends seeing her and Luke together... like that. "So much has happened in the last month," she said, trying to change the subject before either of them mentioned her father's wedding again. "Who'd ever have believed Luke would end up buying the ranch?"

"I know it must have come as a shock to you," Clay said evenly, "but I've been after him for years to get his own spread."

"What are your plans now that the Circle L's been sold?" Rorie wanted to know.

"I'm looking for a place in town," she explained, and sipped her wine.

"From what Luke told me, he'd rather you continued living on the ranch," Clay said, studying her as though he knew something she didn't.

"I know," Kate admitted. "It's really very generous of him, but I'd prefer to get an apartment of my own."

"Good luck finding one," Clay murmured.

They were both aware that a decent apartment might be difficult to locate. Nightingale was a place of family dwellings, not singles' apartments.

They chatted easily as they waited for Mary to announce dinner. Every now and again Kate saw Clay glance over at Rorie. His look was tender and warm and filled with the deep joy that comes from loving completely and knowing that love is returned.

When Rorie Campbell had arrived in their midst, Kate realized almost immediately that Clay was attracted to her. That was understandable, after all, since Rorie was a beautiful woman. In the beginning, Kate had done everything she could to combat her jealousy. Rorie had been due to leave Elk Run in a few days and once she was gone, Kate had told herself, their lives and feelings would return to normal.

Eventually Rorie did return to San Francisco, but Clay wasn't able to forget her. Kate had done her best to pretend; she'd even talked Clay into setting a wedding date, pressuring him in a not-so-subtle way to marry her quickly. They'd been talking about it for years, and Kate wanted the deed done before Rorie realized what she'd given up when she'd left Clay. Their getting married seemed the perfect solution. Then, if Rorie did decide to return to Nightingale, it would be too late.

Kate's strategy had been a desperate one, planned by a desperate woman. And as often happens in such cases, her scheme backfired.

Kate didn't think she'd ever forget the day Clay told her he wanted to break their engagement. The words had scarred her soul like lye on tender skin. He'd come to the ranch, and from the minute he'd asked to talk to her, Kate had known something was terribly wrong. She'd tried to fill the tension with talk of bridesmaids' dresses and floral arrangements, but Clay had stopped her.

He'd sat with his hands folded, his eyes regarding her sadly. "I wouldn't hurt you for the world," he'd said, and his words rang with truth and regret.

"Clay, you could never hurt me." Which was a lie, because he was already inflicting pain.

He'd told her then, simply and directly, that it would be wrong for them to marry. Not once did he mention Rorie's name. He didn't need to. Kate had known for weeks that Clay was in love with the other woman. But she'd chosen instead to involve her heart in a painful game of pretend.

Instead of accepting the truth when Clay had come to her with his decision, she'd insisted he was wrong, that they *were* right for each other and had been all their lives. The memory humbled her now. She'd tried to convince him that all they needed was a little more time. By the next week, or maybe the next month, Clay would realize he'd made a mistake and would want to go through with the wedding. She could afford to be patient because she loved him so much. Kindly, and as gently as possible, Clay had told her time wouldn't alter the way he felt. Then he'd left, although she'd pleaded with him to stay.

In the week that followed, Kate had felt as though she were walking around in a thick fog. She laughed, she smiled, she slept, she ate. The school year hadn't started yet, so there was little else to occupy her mind. The days bled into each other, one indistinguishable from the next.

As Kate had known, Clay, soon after he'd broken their engagement, headed for San Francisco, purportedly to attend a horse show. In her heart, she'd expected Clay left to return with Rorie at his side. As hard as it had been, she'd tried to accept the fact Clay loved Rorie and nothing was ever going to change that.

To everyone's surprise, Clay returned home alone, and there was no mention of Rorie. Kate didn't know what had happened between them. Hope stirred in her chest, and she'd briefly entertained thoughts of Clay resuming their engagement, the two of them marrying and settling down together, the way she'd always dreamed.

Instead she stood helplessly by as Clay threw himself into his work, making unreasonable demands on himself and his men. At first she believed the situation would change. She began stopping off at Elk Run, trying to be the friend she knew Clay needed. But Clay didn't want her. He didn't want anyone.

Except Rorie.

Only then did Kate understand that it was in her power to help this man she loved. She talked over her idea with Luke, even before she approached her father. Luke, and Luke alone, had seemed to understand and appreciate her sacrifice. When she couldn't hold back the tears any longer, it had been Luke who'd held her in his arms and who'd beamed with pride over the unselfishness of her deed.

As she sat, listening to the predinner conversation, even contributing now and then, she realized that Luke had been the one who'd helped her survive that most difficult time.

Luke.

Losing Clay had threatened to destroy her mentally and physically. But Luke hadn't allowed that to happen. It was then he'd started bullying her, she realized. She'd thought of him as a tyrant, with his unreasonable demands and his gentle harassments. At the time, Kate had been so furious with him for assuming command of her life that she'd overlooked the obvious. Only now could she understand and appreciate his strategy. Gradually, the fire had returned to her eyes and her life, although it had been fueled by indignation. Nevertheless it was there, and Luke had been the person responsible.

She'd been furious with him when she should have been grateful. Luke had never stopped being her friend—the best friend she'd ever had. She'd leaned heavily on him in the days and weeks before Clay married Rorie, though she had never understood how much he'd done for her, how much he cared.

The wineglasses were replenished and Kate proposed a toast. "To your happiness," she said sincerely. It pained Kate to realize Clay and Rorie had nearly lost each other. Because of her...

Nightingale had needed a librarian, and with her father's help, Kate had convinced the town council to offer the job to Rorie Campbell. When she'd turned them down, Kate herself had called Rorie, and together they'd wept over the phone and later in each other's arms.

So Rorie had returned to Nightingale, and she and Clay had been married. In October. The same month Kate had planned for her own wedding to Clay.

Kate's thoughts were pulled back to the present when Clay said, "Rorie has a piece of good news." He cast a proud look at his wife.

"What's that?" Kate asked.

Rorie blushed becomingly. "Clay shouldn't have said anything. It's not for certain yet."

"Rorie," Kate said, studying her carefully, "you're not pregnant so soon, are you? Why, that's wonderful!"

"No, no." Rorie rushed to correct the impression. "Good grief, we've been married less than a month."

"It's about Rorie's book," Clay explained.

Vaguely Kate remembered that Rorie wrote children's books. In fact, she'd been on her way to a writers' conference when the car she was driving broke down on the road not far from Elk Run.

"Has one of your stories been accepted for publication?" Kate asked eagerly.

"Not exactly," Rorie said.

"An editor from New York phoned and asked for a few revisions, but she sounded enthusiastic about the book and there was some talk of a contract once the revisions are done," Clay said. His fingers were twined with his wife's and he looked as excited as if he'd created the story himself.

"Oh, Rorie, that's wonderful." Kate felt pleased and proud for her friend. "What's the book about?"

"Well, the story involves Star Bright and the night we delivered Nightsong, and it's told from the foal's point of view," Rorie said.

"I know I'm her husband," Clay broke in, "but I read it, and I don't mind telling you, the book's gripping. Any editor worth her salt would snap it up in a minute."

"Oh, Clay, honestly!"

"When will you know if it's sold?" Kate wanted to know. "I don't think Nightingale's ever had an author living here before. Dad could convince the town council to commission a sign so folks would know. You might even become a tourist attraction. Who knows what this could turn into?''

They all laughed, but Rorie cautioned, "It could be months yet before I hear a word, so don't go having your father commission any signs.''

"You should have seen her after the call arrived,'' Clay said, his eyes twinkling with merriment. "I didn't know what to think. Rorie came running out of the house and started shrieking and jumping up and down.''

"So I was a little excited.''

Playfully Clay rolled his eyes. "A little! That's got to be the understatement of the year.''

"I'd behave the same way,'' Kate defended. "And you seem pretty thrilled about all this yourself, Clay Franklin.''

Clay admitted it, and then the discussion turned to the awards Clay had accumulated in several national horse shows this past year.

A few minutes later, Mary announced that dinner was ready and they moved into the dining room. The meal was lively, and conversation flowed easily around the table.

Kate had been dreading this dinner almost from the moment Rorie had issued the invitation. Now she was pleasantly surprised by how enjoyable the evening had become. She'd been convinced that seeing Clay and Rorie's happiness would deepen her own pain. It hadn't happened. She'd expected to spend this evening nursing her wounds behind a brave front. Instead she felt almost giddy with a sense of release.

She *had* loved Clay, she realized, loved him with a youthful innocence. But she didn't feel the same way toward him now. Clay belonged to Rorie and Rorie to him. The tender relationship Kate had once shared with him was part of the past. He would always be a special person in her life, but those old feelings, that adulation she'd felt for him, were relegated to her adolescent fantasies.

Kate Logan was a woman now.

She wasn't sure exactly when the transformation had taken place, but it had. She'd struggled with it, fought the metamorphosis, because change, as always, was both painful and difficult. Kate realized for the first time that all the pain, all the uncertainty, had not been for nothing.

"KATE?" LUKE CALLED, as he let himself into the house. "You around?"

"In here." She was at the back of the house, packing away the library of books her father kept in his den. Every night she did a little more to get the main house ready for Luke to move in and her to move out.

She straightened up and tucked in a few wisps of hair that had escaped the red bandana. She wore blue jeans and an old gray sweatshirt and no doubt looked terrible. Despite that, she was pleased to see Luke, eager to talk to him. She was wiping her dusty palms on her jeans when he walked in.

"What are you doing?" He stood just inside the door, a dark frown creasing his forehead.

"What does it look like?" she said. "I'm packing."

He hesitated, then said, "I told you, I want you to live here, at least to the end of the school year. I thought you understood that."

"I do, Luke. It's just that this place is yours now— or will be soon, and there's no reason for me to stay on." For one despairing moment, she was swept away on a crashing wave of disbelief and misery at all she'd lost in so short a time. She could barely walk through her home and not feel an aching throb at the thought of leaving it behind. But the sale of the ranch was part of the new reality she was learning to face.

"Of course there's a reason for you to stay here," Luke insisted, his voice sharp with impatience. "It's where you belong—where I want you. Isn't that reason enough?"

Kate forced a light laugh. "Honestly, Luke, there's no excuse for me to continue living here. You don't need a housekeeper, or a cook or anything else. As I recall, you're completely self-sufficient. And I could do without all the gossip my living here would start in town." She paused a moment, then added gently, "I really *can* manage on my own, you know. I'm a big girl, Luke, and I don't need anyone to take care of me."

He wanted to argue with her; Kate could sense it with every breath he drew. But when he spoke next, his remarks had nothing to do with her moving.

"I suppose I should tell you about the feed store," he said. His voice was controlled, though Kate heard a hint of steel in his words. He'd been just as angry as she was over the incident. Once she'd come to grips with her own outrage, she'd recognized how furious Luke was.

"No...well, yes, I guess I am curious to know how you handled that. Would you like some coffee?"

"Please."

Kate led the way into the kitchen and filled two ceramic mugs. After handing Luke his, she moved into the living room and sat on the sofa. Relaxing, she slipped off her shoes and tucked her feet underneath her. It felt good to sit here with Luke—almost like old times. So often over the years, they'd sat and talked like this. Friends. Confidants. Companions. She cradled the mug in both hands, letting the warmth seep up her arms.

"I had dinner with Clay and Rorie last night," she said, wanting to share with Luke what she'd discovered.

"Yes, I heard. Listen, I want you to know you can close the door on the situation with Fred Garner. You don't need to worry about it anymore."

Kate lowered her gaze. "Thanks," she murmured. There was so much she wanted to tell Luke. "I had a great time at Elk Run last night, though I honestly didn't expect to."

"I can personally guarantee the matter with Garner is over. If it isn't a dead issue, it soon will be."

Kate didn't want to talk about the wedding lottery. The subject had become an embarrassing memory—a very embarrassing one—but as Luke said, it was finished. There were other, far more important issues to discuss.

Since her evening with Clay and Rorie, Kate had been doing a lot of serious thinking. For weeks, she'd been abrupt and impatient with Luke and only in the past twenty-four hours had she realized how grateful she should be to him. He'd helped her through the most difficult weeks of her life in ways she was only beginning to understand.

"All day I'd worried about that dinner," she said, starting over. "I wondered how I'd ever be able to sit at a table with Clay, knowing he was married to Rorie. But I did. Oh, Luke, I can't tell you how happy they are. Deep down, I knew they would be, and I had to brace myself for that, expecting to find it unbearably painful. But something incredible happened, something wonderful. During the evening, I learned a valuable lesson about—"

"Good." Luke's response was clipped, detached.

Kate hesitated. From the moment he'd walked into her father's office, she'd felt something was wrong, but she hadn't been able to put her finger on it. "Luke, what is it?"

"Nothing. I'd prefer not talking about Clay and Rorie, all right?"

"I . . . suppose so," she said, feeling hurt. After an awkward moment, she attempted conversation once more. "You'll never guess who I got a letter from today." If Luke didn't want to talk about Clay and Rorie, then she'd try another topic that was sure to pique his interest. "Eric Wilson. Remember him?"

A slight smile touched Luke's mouth. "I'm not likely to forget him. What'd he have to say?"

"He's moved back to Portland and is talking to his ex-wife. Apparently she's been just as miserable as he has since their divorce. It looks like they might get back together."

"That's good news."

"He asked me to give you his regards, and sends his thanks." Kate paused. "But he didn't say what I was to thank you for?'' She made the statement a question, hoping Luke would supply an answer.

"We talked once."

"Oh," Kate returned, disappointed.

"I told him he was wasting his time on you because you're in love with me."

Kate was outraged. "Luke, you didn't! Please tell me you're joking."

He smiled briefly, then his eyes took on the distant look he'd been wearing a moment earlier. Kate couldn't ignore it any longer. "Luke, please, tell me what's bothering you."

"What makes you think anything is?"

"You don't seem yourself tonight." Something in his voice puzzled her. A reserved quality. It was as if he was distancing himself from her and that was baffling. After Clay's wedding, Luke had actually insisted they marry and now he was treating her like some casual acquaintance. She didn't know what to think.

Kate took another sip of coffee while she collected her thoughts. Luke was sitting as far away from her as he could and still be in the same room. His shoulders were straight and stiff and his dark eyes a shade more intense than she could remember. Gone was the laughing devilry she adored.

"I'll be out of town for a few days next week," he said stiffly. "I'm hoping to pick up a few pieces of new equipment from a wholesaler in New Mexico."

"When will the bank close the deal on the ranch?"

Luke paused and his eyes pinned hers. "Your father and I signed all the necessary papers the day before he married Dorothea Murphy."

Kate felt like bolting from the chair, the shock was so great. "Why didn't you say something?" she demanded, her heart racing. "Why didn't my father? I shouldn't even be here now. This is your home. Yours. Bought and paid for and—"

"Kate." He set his mug aside and wearily rubbed the back of his neck. "You're welcome to stay as long as you need. If you insist on leaving, that's fine, too, but there's no rush."

She brought her hands to her cheeks, which were feverishly hot one minute, numb and cold the next. "I'll be out as . . . as soon as I can find some place to move."

"Kate, for the love of heaven, why do you persist in being so stubborn?"

She shook her head, hardly understanding it herself. All she knew was that this place, which had been a part of her from the time she was born, no longer belonged to her family. Despite everything Luke said, she couldn't stay on at the Circle L, and she had no other place to go.

CHAPTER EIGHT

KATE HAD JUST FINISHED correcting a pile of math papers when her friend, Linda Hutton, strolled into her classroom. Linda's third-grade class had been on a field trip and the two friends had missed talking at lunch.

"Hi," Kate said, smiling up at her. "How'd the tour of the jail and fire station go?"

Linda pulled up a child-size chair and sank heavily down on it, then started massaging her temples with her fingertips. "Don't ask. By noon I was ready to lock up the entire third-grade class and lose the key."

"It certainly was quiet around school."

Linda gave a soft snicker. "Listen, I didn't come in here to learn what a peaceful day *you* had. The only reason I'm not home in bed curled up with aspirin and a hot-water bottle is so I can tell you I was at Garner Feed and Supply yesterday afternoon."

"Oh?"

"Yes, and you aren't going to like what happened. While I was there, Mr. Garner asked me if I wanted to place a wager on the Rivers-Logan wedding."

Kate's heart stopped cold. "He didn't!"

"I'm afraid so."

"But Luke told me he'd taken care of the problem. He said it was a dead issue and that I shouldn't worry about it any longer." It wasn't like Luke to make careless promises.

"I wish I didn't have to tell you this," Linda said, with a sympathetic sigh.

"But Luke told me he'd personally talked to Fred Garner."

"He did. Mr. Garner made a point of telling me that, too," Linda confirmed. "He claimed Luke was hotter than a Mexican chili pepper. Said Luke came into his place, ranted and raved and threatened him within an inch of his life. But, Kate, I'm telling you the whole time old Garner was talking to me he wore a grin so wide I could have driven a Jeep through it."

Kate sagged against the back of her chair.

"Then Mr. Garner started telling me that the harder a man fights marriage, the faster he falls. From what he said, he's taking bets from as far away as Riversdale and southward."

Kate pressed a hand over her eyes. "What am I going to do now?"

Linda shook her head. "I don't know. At least Garner's taken it off the blackboard, but when I said something about that, he told me he had to, since half the county wants in on the action. Apparently the betting outgrew his blackboard space."

"If nothing else it all proves how desperate this community is for entertainment," Kate returned stiffly. "If the good people of Nightingale have nothing better to do than waste their time and money betting on something as silly as a wedding date, then it's a sad commentary on our lives here."

Kate's friend cleared her throat, and looked suspiciously guilty.

Kate hesitated, studying Linda. No, she mused, her gaze narrowing. Not Linda. Her closest childhood friend wouldn't place a wager. Her expression confirmed that she would.

"You chose a date yourself, didn't you?" Kate demanded.

Linda's gaze bounced all over the room, avoiding Kate's completely.

"You did, didn't you?" Kate exclaimed, hardly able to believe Linda would do such a thing.

Linda's fingers were curling and uncurling in her lap. "You're my oldest, dearest friend. How could I ever do anything like that?" she wailed.

"I don't know, Linda. You tell me."

"All right, all right," Linda confessed. "I did put a wager on June. The first part of summer is such a lovely time of year for a wedding and you'd make a beautiful bride."

"I can't believe I'm hearing this." Kate had the sinking suspicion that her father had probably gotten in on the action, too, before he left for his honeymoon.

"I had no intention of betting," Linda hurried to explain. "In fact I never would have, but the odds were so good for June. For a five-dollar bet, I could collect as much as five hundred in return if you were to marry around the middle of the month—say the sixteenth. It's a Saturday. Weekends are always best for weddings, don't you think?"

Kate wasn't about to answer that. "You know, I think this whole thing is illegal. Each and every one of you should thank your lucky stars I don't call the sheriff."

"He's betting himself—on March. Said his own wedding anniversary is March tenth and he thinks Luke will be able to persuade you early in the spring. According to Fred, the sheriff thinks once Luke gets you to agree, he won't wait around for a big wedding. He'll want to marry you before you can change your mind."

Kate gave her a furious look. "If you're telling me all this to amuse me, you've failed miserably."

"I'm sorry, Kate, I really am. The only reason I went into the feed store was so I could assure you the whole thing was over, only I can't and—"

"Instead you placed a wager of your own."

"I feel guilty enough about that," Linda admitted, her voice subdued.

"Why don't we both forget the whole thing and concentrate on the Thanksgiving play?" Instead of upsetting herself with more talk of this wedding lottery, Kate preferred to do something constructive with her time.

"I think I may be able to make it up to you, though," Linda murmured, fussing with the cuffs of her long-sleeved blouse.

"Whatever it is will have to be good."

"It is." Linda brightened and pulled a slip of paper from her purse. "I got this information from a friend of a friend, so I don't know how accurate it is, but I think it's pretty much for sure."

"What's for sure?" she asked when Linda handed her the paper. A local phone number was carefully printed on it.

Linda's sheepish look departed. "It's Mrs. Jackson's number—she's the manager of the apartment complex on Spruce Street. They may have a vacancy coming up early next week. If you're the first one to apply, you might have a decent chance of getting it."

"Oh, Linda, that's great."

"Am I forgiven?"

Kate laughed. "This makes up for a multitude of sins."

"I was counting on that."

KATE CALLED FIVE TIMES before she was able to get through. Mrs. Jackson seemed surprised to be hearing from her.

"I thought you were marrying that Rivers chap," the elderly woman said. "Can't understand why you'd want to rent an apartment when you're engaged to that man. The whole town says it's just a matter of time."

"Mrs. Jackson," Kate said loudly, because everyone knew the older woman was hard of hearing, "could I look at the apartment soon?"

"Won't be cleaned up for another day or two. I'll let you know once it's ready to be shown, but I can't help feeling it's a waste of time. Don't know what's wrong with you young women these days. In my time, we'd snap up a good man like Luke Rivers so fast it'd make your head spin."

"I'd still like to see the apartment," Kate pressed.

"Saturday, I guess. Yes, Saturday. Why don't you plan to come over then? I'll need a deposit if you decide to take the place."

"Will a check be all right?"

"Good as gold when it's got your name on it," the older woman said, chuckling. "Don't suppose you have any season or month that you're particularly partial to for weddings, would you?"

"No, I can't say that I do."

"Well, me and Ethel Martin think you and that Rivers fellow will tie the knot in April. April seems a mighty nice month for a country wedding."

"I'm sure it is," Kate said, clenching her teeth.

"Good. Now listen, soon as the word gets out, someone else will be wanting that apartment, so if you aren't here by noon Saturday, I'm afraid I'm going to have to give it to whoever else shows up. You understand?"

"I'll be there before noon."

"I'll look forward to seeing you then."

"Goodbye, Mrs. Jackson."

"You keep thinking about April, you hear?"

"Yes, I will," Kate murmured, rolling her eyes as she replaced the receiver.

That night, Luke stopped in shortly after Kate had finished dinner, which consisted of a sandwich eaten while she emptied the living room bookcases. She filled box after box with books, her own and her father's, as well as complete sets of Dickens, Thackeray, and George Eliot that had belonged to her mother. The physical activity gave her time to think. She'd realized the night she had dinner at the Franklins' that she wasn't in love with Clay. That same evening, Kate had also realized how much Luke had done for her in the weeks following her broken engagement. It troubled her to acknowledge how unappreciative she'd been of his support.

At Clay's wedding, she'd only added to the problem by asking Luke to marry her. He'd been willing to comply, willing to continue taking care of her through these difficult emotional times. In his own way, he did love her; Kate didn't doubt that. But he seemed far more concerned about protecting her from the harsh realities of life.

All the talk about weddings had brought the subject to the forefront of Kate's mind. She tried to picture what her life would be like if she were to marry Luke. From the night of Clay's wedding, Luke had been telling her she was in love with him. It came as a shock to her to realize how right he was. She did love him, a thousand times more than she'd ever dreamed.

Luke claimed he loved her, too. If that was true, then why was she fighting him so hard? For one thing, Luke had delivered any declaration of love in such a matter-of-fact, unromantic way, it was hard to believe he really meant it. He seemed to prefer forcing her into admitting she loved him. If she could be sure that his feelings were rooted in something more than sympathy and a strong physical attraction, she would feel more confident. But Luke kept trying to shield her, as though she were a child. Now that she was moving into a place of her own, she'd be able to analyze her changing feelings more objectively. She'd be completely on her own, away from the environment they'd always shared. Once they were apart, once it was clear that she could manage on her own, Luke would be free to pursue a relationship with her as an equal, an adult woman—not a little girl who needed looking after.

"I see you're at it again," he said, standing in the doorway between the kitchen and the living room.

"Luke—" she slapped her hand over her heart "—you startled me!" Her thoughts had been full of him and then suddenly he was there.

As he did more and more often of late, Luke was frowning, but Kate wasn't going to let that destroy her mood. She was thrilled with the prospect of moving into her own apartment and settling into a different kind of life.

"I have good news. I'm going to look at an apartment Saturday morning." She dragged a heavy box of books across the carpet. "So," she said, huffing, "I'll probably be out of here sooner than we thought."

Luke interrupted her, effortlessly picking up the cardboard box and depositing it on the growing stack at the far side of the room.

"Thanks," she murmured, grateful for his help.

"You shouldn't be doing this heavy work on your own."

"It's no problem," she countered, rubbing the dust from her hands. "The only trouble I'm having is with these books. I didn't realize we had so many."

"Kate, dammit, I wish you'd listen to reason."

"I'm being reasonable," she said, fixing a reassuring smile on her face. "The only thing I'm doing is giving you what's rightly yours."

Luke's frown grew darker, and he dragged a hand through his hair. "Listen, I think we may have more of a problem with Fred Garner than I first realized."

"Yes, I know," Kate said, already filling the next box. "Linda told me after school that he's doing a thriving business."

Luke knelt on the floor beside her. "You're not upset?"

"Would it do any good? I mean, you obviously did your best and that only seemed to encourage the betting. As far as I can see, the only thing that will settle this issue is time." She kept her gaze averted and added, "When six months pass and we're still not married, most everyone will accept that nothing's going on between us.''

"Nothing?'' Luke asked bitterly.

Hope stirred briefly within her. "I like to think we'll always be friends.'' An absent smile touched her lips. "Now that I've decided to distance my emotions from this silly lottery business, I find it all rather comical. I think you should do the same.''

"This whole thing amuses you?''

"The good citizens of Nightingale are amused, I suppose. Everyone seems to assume that because Clay and Dad both got married and the ranch has been sold, I should swoon into your arms.''

"Personally, I don't think that's such a bad idea.''

"Oh?'' She chuckled and tucked a few more books in the box. Her heart was racing. If Luke was ever really going to declare his love, it would be now. "That wasn't the message I got the other night. I tried to have a serious talk with you about my evening with Clay and Rorie, and all you could do was glower at me.'' She glanced up at him and gently shook her head. "Like you're doing now.''

Luke walked away from her. He stood staring out the window, although Kate suspected the view was of little interest to him. "I just wish you'd be sensible for once in your life,'' he snapped.

"I didn't know I had a habit of not being sensible,'' she said conversationally, disheartened by his attitude. She rose and walked over to the larger bookcase, but even standing on the tips of her toes, she couldn't quite reach the trophies stored on the top shelf. Not to be defeated, she rolled the ottoman in front of the empty bookcase and climbed onto the thick cushioned seat. She stretched up and her fingers were just about to grasp the first trophy when she heard Luke's swift intake of breath.

"Kate, good Lord . . ."

Just as he spoke the ottoman started to roll out from under her feet. She flailed her arms in a desperate effort to maintain her balance.

Kate had never seen Luke move faster. His hands closed around her waist in an iron grip. Her cry of alarm caught in her throat as she was forcefully slammed against his solid chest.

"Of all the stupid, idiotic things I've ever seen—"

"I would have been perfectly fine if you hadn't called my name." Her heart was pounding so hard she could barely breathe.

Luke's hold relaxed. "You're all right?"

"Fine."

He closed his eyes, exhaling a ragged sigh. When he opened them, he assessed her carefully; he apparently concluded that she was unhurt because he gave her an impatient little shake. "Whatever possessed you to climb up on that ottoman in the first place?" he demanded.

"I couldn't reach the trophies."

"Couldn't you have asked me to get them for you? Why do you have such a difficult time accepting help from me?"

"I don't know," she admitted softly.

Still he held her and still Kate let him, trying to resist the comfort she felt in his arms. Her hands were braced against his powerful shoulders, but then she relaxed, unconsciously linking her fingers behind his neck.

Neither moved for a long moment.

Slowly Luke ran a provocative finger down the length of her cheek, and Kate's eyes drifted shut. She felt herself drawn inexorably toward him. Her lips parted and trembled, awaiting his kiss. When she realized what she was doing, her eyes snapped open and she broke away from him with such force that she would have stumbled had his hands not righted her.

Embarrassed now, she stepped back. Luke brought down the trophies and handed them to her, but she noted that his eyes had become distant and unreadable.

"I think that's enough packing for tonight," she murmured, her voice breathless even while she struggled to sound cheerful and bright.

He nodded slightly, then without another word, stalked from the room. Kate didn't know what possessed her to follow him, certainly the last thing she should have done.

"Luke?"

He stopped halfway through the kitchen and turned toward her. His eyes were steely and intense, and just seeing that harsh edge in them drove her to take a step backward in retreat.

"You wanted something?" he asked when she didn't immediately explain.

"Just to say..." She could barely talk coherently. It occurred to her to ask if he loved her the way a man loves his wife, but she lacked the courage. "I thought maybe, I mean, I wanted to know if there was anything I could do for you before I left the house. Paint the living room ... or something?"

"No."

Briefly she toyed with the idea of following him outside. For all his words about wanting her to stay, he couldn't seem to get away from her fast enough. The thought of not having Luke for her friend anymore felt almost crippling. Her pride was the problem. Luke had told her repeatedly that she needed him, and she knew now that she did. But not in the way he meant. Not just as a friend who was willing to offer her the protection and peace of marriage, a friend who felt obliged to take care of her.

"I don't want you to move from the ranch," he said.

Her heart was begging him to give her a reason to stay—the reason she longed to hear. "Luke, please accept that I'm only doing what I think is best in my life."

"I realize that, but dammit, Kate, you're being so stubborn it's all I can do to remain sane. Why do you resist me when all I want to do is make things easier for you? We could be married, and you could settle down in the house, and nothing need change. Yet you insist on causing all this turmoil in your life."

There wasn't anything Kate could say.

"You can't tell me we aren't physically attracted to each other. The electricity between us is powerful enough to light up Main Street."

"I . . . know."

"Say it, Kate. Admit that it felt good to have me hold you just now."

"I . . ."

When Luke reached for her, Kate felt as if she'd lost some strategic battle. When his mouth found hers, her stomach tightened and fluttered wildly. Against her will, her lips parted, and before she realized what was happening, she slid her arms tightly around his hard, narrow waist, wanting to hold on to him forever.

Luke moaned, then suddenly tore his lips away from hers. She felt a tremor go through him before he raised his head and gazed tenderly into her face, his eyes dark and gentle.

"Is it so difficult to say?" he asked.

CHAPTER NINE

"THIS IS THE SECOND BEDROOM," Mrs. Jackson was saying as she led Kate through the vacant apartment. From the moment she'd walked in the door, Kate had known that this place would suit her needs perfectly.

"I can't understand why you'd be wanting a two-bedroom place, but that's none of my business," Mrs. Jackson went on. Her hair was tightly curled in pink plastic rollers. To the best of her ability, Kate couldn't remember ever seeing the woman's hair *without* rollers.

"What did that Rivers fellow say when you told him you were moving into town?" She didn't wait for a response, but cackled delightedly, contemplating the thought. "Frankly, I wasn't sure you'd show this morning. My friend Ethel and me talked about it, and we thought Rivers would tie a rope around you and hightail it to Nevada and marry you quick. Offhand, I can't remember who's got money on November."

"I was determined to be here before noon," she said, ignoring the other comments.

"So I see. If Luke didn't stop you, I expected that snowstorm the weatherman's been talking about for the past two days would."

"Do you really think it's going to snow?" Kate asked anxiously. The sky had been dark all morning, and the temperature seemed to be dropping steadily.

Normally Kate wouldn't have chanced driving into town by herself with weather conditions this uncertain, but if she hadn't come, she might have missed getting the apartment.

"If I was you, I'd stick around town for a while," Mrs. Jackson advised. "I'd hate the thought of you getting trapped on the road in a bad storm."

"I'm sure I'll be all right." She'd driven her father's four-wheel-drive truck, and even if the storm did hit, she shouldn't have much trouble getting home. The Circle L was only twenty minutes away, and how much snow could settle in that time? Not much, she decided.

"Would you like me to write you a check now?" Kate asked, eager to be on her way.

"That would be fine. There's still some cleaning to be done, but I'll make sure it's finished before the first of the month. Fact is, you can start moving your things in here next week if you want."

"Thanks, I appreciate that."

Mrs. Jackson bundled her coat around her thin shoulders as they stepped outside. She glanced at the sky and shook her pink curlered head. "If you're going home, I'd suggest you do it quick. I don't like the look of them clouds. They seem downright angry to me."

"If that's the case, I'd better write that check and hurry home."

No more than five minutes later, Kate was sitting inside her father's truck. The sky was an oyster gray and darkening by the minute. Shivering from the cold, she zipped her jacket all the way up to her neck and drew on a pair of fur-lined leather gloves.

Kate started the engine and shifted the gears. The radio was set on her dad's favorite country station and the music played softly, giving her a sense of peace. When she left the outskirts of town, she hit a couple of rough patches in the road and bounced so high her head nearly hit the roof of the cab. After that she kept her speed down. She drove at a steady pace, her gaze focused on the road ahead, scanning the horizon for any sign of snow.

When she was about ten miles from the ranch, the storm hit. Light, fluffy flakes whirled around the windshield. The morning sky darkened until it resembled dusk and Kate was forced to turn on the headlights.

A love song came on the radio, one the band at the Red Bull had played that fateful Friday night. The night Luke had lifted her in his arms and carried her off the dance floor. Embarrassed by the memory, she reached for the radio dial, intending to change to station.

She didn't see the rock that had rolled onto the roadway, not until she was on top of it, and then it was too late. Her instincts took control. She gripped the wheel with both hands, then swerved and slammed into the embankment. The truck stopped with a sudden jerk, and the engine went dead.

For a stunned moment, Kate couldn't so much as breathe. Her heart was in her throat and her hands clenched the steering wheel so tightly her fingers felt numb.

Finally, when she was able to move, Kate released a long, slow breath, grateful the accident hadn't been worse. She took a moment to compose herself and tried to restart the engine, but nothing happened.

Twice more she tried to get the engine to kick over, but it wouldn't even cough or sputter.

Frustrated, she smacked the cushioned seat with her gloved hand and closed her eyes. The snow was coming down thick and fast now.

"Don't worry," she muttered, opening the door and climbing out. "Stay calm." Although everything Kate knew about the internal workings of engines would fit in a thimble, she decided to take a look to see if she could find the problem.

The snow and wind slapped at her viciously, as though to punish her for not listening to Mrs. Jackson and staying in town.

After considerable difficulty finding the latch, Kate lifted the hood. With a prayer on her lips, she looked everything over, then touched two or three different parts as if that would repair whatever was broken. Certain that she was destined to sit out the storm huddled in the cab, she returned and tried the key once more.

The engine gave one sick cough and promptly died.

"Damn!"

Nothing remained but to sit and wait for someone to drive past. Leaving the truck and attempting to find her way to the house would be nearly as insane as driving around in a snowstorm in the first place.

Kate could almost hear Luke's lecture now. It would be hot enough to blister her ears. All she could do was hope her father never found out about this—or she'd have a lecture from him, too.

A half hour passed and, hoping against hope, Kate tried the engine again. Nothing. But it was snowing so hard now that even if the truck had started, she probably wouldn't have been able to drive in these conditions. She tried to warm herself by rubbing her hands together and hugging her arms close to her body. Lord, it was cold, the coldest weather she could remember.

With little to take her mind off the freezing temperatures, she laid her head back and closed her eyes, forcing herself to relax. There was nothing to do but sit patiently and wait....

She must have dozed off because the next thing she knew, the truck door was jerked open and her arm gripped in a sudden, painful grasp.

"Have you lost your mind?" The fury in Luke's voice was like a slap in the face.

"Luke...Luke." She was so grateful to see him that she didn't question where he'd come from or how he'd found her. It all felt like a dream. Moving was difficult, but she slid her arms around his neck and hugged him, laughing and crying at the same time. "How did you ever find me?"

"Good Lord, don't you realized I was about to have heart failure worrying about you?"

"You're sick?" Her mind was so muddled. Of course he'd be worried, and how had he known where she was? And he seemed so angry now, but then, for the past several days he'd been continually upset with her.

Her arms tightened around his neck and she breathed in the fresh, warm scent of him. When she sat up and looked around, she was shocked by how dark it had become; if it weren't for the blowing, swirling snow, the stars would be twinkling. The storm had abated somewhat, but not by much.

"I can't believe you'd do anything so stupid." His voice was low and angry, his face blanched with concern. "Don't you realize you could have frozen to death out here? If you don't want to consider your own life or what you might have suffered as a result of your impulsiveness, then what about Devin away on his honeymoon? If anything happened to you, he'd never forgive himself."

Kate bore up well under Luke's tirade, refusing to cry even though she was trembling with shock and cold and the truth of his words. As for the part about being frozen, she was already halfway there, but he didn't seem to notice that.

"Kate, I don't know what I would have done if you'd left the truck and tried to make it back to the house on foot."

"I knew enough to stay here at least." She'd been a fool not to have taken the danger more seriously. "I'm sorry," she whispered.

He pulled her to him and held her so tight she couldn't move. His face was buried in her hair, one ungloved hand gently stroking her forehead, her cheek, her chin, as if he had to touch her to know he'd found her safe. When he lifted his head, he roughly brushed the hair from her face and gazed into her eyes, his own dark and filled with unspoken torment. "Are you all right?"

She nodded and tried to talk, but her teeth started to chatter. Luke shrugged out of his coat and draped it over her shoulders.

"Tell me what happened."

"I swerved to miss a rock and hit...something. It had already started to snow and I...the song...I changed stations and that's when it happened...I don't know what I did, but after I turned so sharply, the truck wouldn't start."

"I've got to get you back to the house." He half carried her to his truck and placed her in the passenger seat. He climbed into the driver's side and leaned over to wrap a warm blanket around her, then he reached for her hand and began to rub some warmth back into her fingers.

"What about Dad's truck?" Kate asked, shocked by how tired and weak she felt.

"We'll worry about that later. I'll send someone to fix it when the storm's over."

The blast from the heater felt like a tropical wind and Kate finally started to relax. She was terribly cold but dared not let Luke know.

All the way back to the ranch he didn't say a word. Driving was difficult at best, and she didn't want to disturb his concentration. So she sat beside him, her hands and feet numb despite the almost oppressive warmth, and her eyes heavy with weariness.

Several of the ranch hands ran toward the front porch when Luke pulled into the yard. Kate found the flurry of activity all centered on her disconcerting, but she tried to thank everyone and apologized profusely for the concern she'd caused.

If Luke had been impatient and demanding when he rescued her, it couldn't compare to the way he rapped out orders once she was inside the house.

"A bath," he said, pointing toward the bathroom as if she'd never been there before. "Warm water, not hot."

Bill Schmidt, Luke's newly appointed foreman, followed them to the doorway of the tiny room, looking pale and anxious. Kate felt so weak that she simply stood, leaning against the sink, while Luke ran the bathwater, testing it several times to check the temperature.

"It's stopped snowing. Do you think I should contact one of her female friends? Maybe Mizz Franklin?" Bill asked, shifting awkwardly from foot to foot. When Luke nodded, Bill charged out of the house, slamming the door behind him.

Luke turned off the bathwater and straightened. He shook his head, arms limp and at his sides, mouth stern and tight. "Dear Lord, Kate, what could have possessed you to drive in from town during the worst storm of the year? Can you imagine what went through my mind when I was looking for you?"

It took all her strength just to manage a few words. "How'd . . . you know . . . where I was?"

"You told me you were going to town to look at an apartment on Saturday. Remember? When you weren't back after the blizzard hit, I started calling around town until I learned you were renting one of the apartments on Spruce Street. Mrs. Jackson told me she'd warned you herself and that you'd left several hours earlier. Also that she was fond of April because of all the flowers, whatever the hell that means."

"I'm . . . sorry I worried you."

His hands gripped her shoulders and the anguish he'd endured the past few hours was written plainly on his face. The anger and pain in his eyes told her about the panic he'd felt. A rush of emotion crossed his expression and he pulled her close, wrapping his arms around her.

Luke didn't speak for a long moment. Instead, quietly, gently, his hand stroked her hair as he dragged in several deep breaths.

Kate's heart pounded wildly in her chest. She longed to look at him, to gaze into his eyes again. She was puzzled by the intensity she'd seen there. Fear, yes, doubt and anger, too, but there was something more, something deeper she couldn't recognize.

She longed to tell him she loved him, just the way he claimed she did, but the thought didn't make it to her lips. Love was a strange, unpredictable emotion, she'd learned, so painful and difficult. Her eyes held his and she tried to smile, but her mouth wouldn't cooperate.

Her fingertips mapped out the lines of his face, as she strove to reassure him with her touch, when her words couldn't. He captured her wrist and brought her palm to his lips.

She'd just opened her mouth to speak, when Bill Schmidt came crashing into the room. "Rorie Franklin will be over as soon as she can."

"Thanks, Bill," Luke said without looking away from Kate.

"Uh, I'll be leaving, now, if you don't need me."

"Fine. Thanks again for your help."

"No problem. Certainly glad you're all right, Kate." He touched his hat and then was gone.

"Someone should help you out of those clothes," Luke said, half smiling, "and I don't think I should be the one to do it."

"I'm fine. I can undress myself."

Luke didn't seem inclined to challenge her statement. She floated toward the bathroom door and ushered him out, then shut it softly.

Once she started undressing, she discovered that Luke hadn't been too far wrong when he suggested she needed help. By the time she sank into the warm water, she was shivering, exhausted and intensely cold again.

The water felt wonderful although it stung her tender skin. When the prickling sensation left her, she was almost overwhelmed by the sensation of comfort. She sighed deeply, closed her eyes and lay back in the tepid water.

"Kate," Luke called from the other side of the door, "are you okay in there?"

"I'm fine."

"Do you need anything?"

"No," she assured him.

A sudden thought made her bolt upright, gasping. *Luke could have died searching for me.* She squeezed her eyes closed and whispered a prayer of thanks that the events of this traumatic afternoon had turned out as they had.

She must have sobbed because Luke cried out, "What's wrong? It sounds like you're crying."

"You . . . could have died trying to find me."

"I didn't."

"I know," she said hoarsely, biting into her lower lip. "I'm glad. I wouldn't want you to die."

"That's encouraging," he answered with a soft laugh.

Dressed in her flannel pajamas and long robe, her hair hanging wetly against her shoulders, Kate let herself out of the bathroom. She looked like something the cat had proudly dragged onto the porch, but at least she felt better. A thousand times better.

Luke was sitting in the kitchen, nursing a shot glass of whiskey. Kate had very rarely seen Luke drink straight liquor.

"I blame myself," he muttered. "I knew about the storm and didn't warn you."

"Warn me? It wouldn't have done any good. I would have gone into town, anyway. I had to be there before noon if I was going to get the apartment. You couldn't have stopped me, Luke. You know that."

Luke shook his head grimly. "What I can't understand is why moving away from here is so all-fired important that you'd risk your fool neck to do it."

"Mrs. Jackson said she'd have to give the apartment to someone else if I wasn't there."

"She wouldn't have understood if you'd phoned? You had to go look at it in a blizzard?" He urged her into a chair and poured a cup of hot coffee, adding a liberal dose of whiskey before handing her the cup.

"I already told you I couldn't wait," Kate said patiently. "Please don't be angry, Luke." She reached for his hand, needing to touch him.

He gripped her fingers with his own. "Kate, if anything should convince you we ought to get married, this is it. You need me, Princess, can't you see that?" He released her hand to brush the damp curls from her face, then framed her cheek with his index fingers. "How many times do I have to tell you that before you'll believe it?"

"Oh, Luke," she moaned, feeling close to tears.

"I want to take care of you, Kate. What nearly happened today, plus the fiasco with Eric Wilson, should tell you something."

She stared at him, feeling a little lost and disoriented. "There are women in this community, women my age, who already have children." Even as she spoke, she realized she wasn't really making sense.

Luke blinked in confusion. "You want children? Great, so do I. In fact, I'm hoping we'll have several."

"That's not what I meant," Kate said, exasperated. She tried again. "These women don't live with a guardian." Was that clearer? she wondered.

"Of course they don't—they're married," Luke countered sharply.

Kate closed her eyes. "Don't you understand? I'm old enough to be on my own. I don't need someone to protect me."

"We're not discussing your age," Luke snapped.

"You don't love me," she blurted. "You feel sorry for me, that's all. You think because Clay's married to Rorie and . . . and Dad married Dorothea that I don't have anyone. But I do! There's Linda and lots of other friends. I've got a good life. I don't need to get married."

Luke bolted from the chair and walked to the sink, pressing both hands against the edge, hunching his shoulders, his back toward her. He said nothing for several moments and when he finally spoke, his voice was cool, detached. "All I can say is that you must feel a lot more strongly about this than I realized. Apparently you're willing to risk your life to get away from me."

"I didn't go to town knowing I was in any danger," she objected.

"Then leave, Kate. I won't try to keep you any longer, despite the fact that I love you and want to marry you. If you want your independence so badly, then take it."

"Luke, please, you don't love me—not the way you should."

"Oh, and what do you know about that? Obviously nothing."

"I know you keep saying you want to take care of me."

"That's so wrong?"

"Yes. A woman needs more."

"My love and my life are all I've got to offer you, Kate. It's a take-it-or-leave-it proposition."

"That's not fair," she said. "You make it sound as though I'm destined to live my life alone if I don't marry you within the next ten minutes."

Slowly he turned to face her. His eyes were piercing and as dark as she'd ever seen them. "Fine. You've made your choice. I'm not going to stand here arguing with you. It's over between us, Kate. This is the last time we'll talk about marriage."

She tried to say something, but couldn't think coherently. Even if she'd been able to work out her thoughts and give them voice, she doubted Luke was in any mood to listen. He avoided looking at her as he walked out of the house.

A fire was blazing in the fireplace and Kate stretched out on the nearby sofa, intending to mull over Luke's words. But her eyes felt as heavy as her heart, and almost as soon as she laid her head on the pillow, she was asleep.

SOMEONE WORKING IN THE KITCHEN stirred Kate to wakefulness, and when she glanced at her watch, she was shocked to realize she'd slept for almost two hours.

Her heart soared when she thought it must be Luke. He'd been so angry with her earlier, though she supposed his anxiety about finding her in the snowstorm explained his attitude. She hoped they could clear the air between them.

But it wasn't Luke. Instead, Rorie peered into the living room, her eyes gentle and concerned.

"I hope you don't mind. Luke let me in."

"You're always welcome here, Rorie, you know that."

"Bill Schmidt called with an incredible story about your being lost in the storm. I could hardly believe it. Clay drove me over as soon as he could, but to be honest I didn't know who was worse off—you or Luke."

At the mention of his name, Kate lowered her gaze to the multicolored quilt spread across her lap. Idly she smoothed the wrinkles, trying not to think about Luke.

"How are you feeling?"

"I'm okay. I just have a little headache."

"A monster of one from the look of you. I've never seen you this pale."

Kate's hands twisted the fringed edge of the homemade quilt. "Luke was furious with me for going into town—I found an apartment, Rorie. He said it was over between us." She began to cry. "He said he'd be glad when I was gone and that he'd...never bother me again." By the time Kate had finished, her voice was reduced to a hoarse whisper.

"I see," Rorie murmured.

"I don't even know Luke anymore. We used to be able to talk to each other and joke together, but lately we're barely able to discuss anything in a rational manner. I've tried, Rorie, I really have, but Luke makes everything so difficult."

"Men have a habit of doing that sometimes."

"I wanted to tell Luke about the night I had dinner with you and Clay and—" She stopped abruptly when she realized what she'd almost said.

"What about it?" Rorie coaxed.

"It's just that I'd dreaded the evening because I was afraid of being with Clay again. I'm sorry, Rorie, I don't want to upset you, but I loved Clay for a long time, and getting over him was much harder than I ever thought it would be. That is, until the night we were all together." The words came rushing from her. "I saw Clay with you and I assumed I'd experience all this pain, but instead I felt completely free. You're both so happy, and I knew, then and there, that I never loved Clay the way you do. True I adored him for years, but it was more of an adolescent infatuation. Clay was a part of my youth. When I realized all these things about myself, all these changes, I felt such hope, such excitement."

"Oh, Kate, I'm so pleased to hear that." A shy smile dented Rorie's cheeks.

"I wanted to explain all this to Luke, but I never got the chance, and now it's all so much worse. I don't know if we'll ever be able to talk to each other again."

"Of course you will."

"But he sounded so angry."

"I'm sure that was because of his concern for your safety."

"I can't talk to him," Kate repeated sadly. "At least not yet, and maybe not for a long time."

"It'll be sooner than you think," Rorie advised. "You won't be able to break off all those years of friendship, and neither will he. He'll be around in a day or two, ready to apologize for being so harsh. Just you wait and see."

Kate shook her head. "You make it all sound so easy."

"Trust me, I know it isn't. When I think back to the way things went between Clay and me, I empathize all the more with what you're going through now."

Kate remembered the dark days following Clay's visit to California. Neither Rorie nor Clay had ever told her what happened. But no one needed to spell it out for her. Clay had gone to San Francisco, intending to bring Rorie back with him, and instead had returned alone.

"Maybe we just need to get away from each other for a while," Kate said. She chewed her lower lip as she considered her own words. "If we aren't in such close proximity, maybe the fog will clear and we'll be able to sort out what we really feel for each other."

"When are you moving to town?"

"Monday," Kate said, looking at the cardboard boxes stacked against the opposite wall.

"Do you need help? Skip, Clay and I could easily lend a hand."

"That would be wonderful."

THE REMAINDER OF THE WEEKEND passed in a blur. Kate didn't see Luke once. So much for Rorie's assurances that he'd be by soon to talk everything out. Apparently he meant everything he'd said.

Monday morning, when she was ready to leave for school, Kate paused before she got into her car, deciding she should at least say goodbye to Luke before she moved out.

Luke wasn't in the barn, but Bill Schmidt was.

"Good morning, Bill."

"Howdy, Kate," he said with a wide grin. "Glad to see there's no ill effects from your accident."

"None, thanks. Is Luke around?"

Bill settled his hands in the pockets of his bib overalls. "No, I thought you knew. He left yesterday afternoon for New Mexico. There's some new equipment there he wants to look at. He won't be back until Thursday."

CHAPTER TEN

KATE WAS CARRYING the last of the cardboard boxes to the dumpster outside the apartment building Thursday evening when she saw Luke's pickup turn onto Spruce Street. He came to a grinding halt at the curb, vaulted out of the cab and stood there scowling at her apartment building. His features were contorted, but for the life of her, Kate couldn't understand why he should be so irritated.

She was about to make her presence known, but before she could act, Luke brought his fist down on the hood. She heard the sound from where she stood. It must have smarted because he rubbed the knuckles for a couple of moments, gazing intently at the red-brick building. Then, tucking his hands in the back pockets of his jeans, he squared his shoulders and strode toward the building. He stopped abruptly, then retreated to his truck. Opening the door, he balanced one foot on the side rail, as if he was about to leap into the cab.

Kate leaned forward on the tips of her toes and stretched out her hand to stop him. It took everything in her not to rush forward, but she didn't trust herself not to burst into tears. Viewing Luke's behavior had moved something deep within her.

If Luke had planned to drive away, he apparently changed his mind, because he slammed the door shut and resolutely faced the apartment building again.

Knowing that the time to make her move was now, Kate casually turned the corner.

"Kate."

"Luke," she said, pretending surprise.

For a moment, Luke didn't say a word. "I just got back to the ranch and discovered that the main house was empty. I thought you'd be there when I returned."

"Mrs. Jackson said I could have the apartment Monday, and since Rorie, Clay and Skip were able to help me move, I couldn't see any reason to delay."

"You might have told me."

Kate lowered her gaze, feeling a little guilty, since they'd parted on such unfriendly terms. "I tried, but you'd already left for New Mexico."

"Bill did say something about you wanting to talk to me," he conceded.

"Would you like to come inside?" she asked, opening the door for him.

"All right." He sounded reluctant.

Once in the apartment they stood looking at each other, and Kate felt terribly awkward. Luke's eyes were dark and luminous and his face had never seemed so dear to her—familiar, yet in some new exciting way, not fully known. She would have liked nothing better than to walk into his arms. She wanted to tell him how sorry she was for the way they'd last parted, to tell him she was ready to accept his proposal on any terms. But her pride made that impossible.

"Nice place you've got here," he said when the silence became painful. He tucked his fingers in his back pockets again.

"Can I take your coat?"

"Please." He took it off and gave it to her.

She motioned toward the sofa. "Would you like to sit down?"

He nodded and sat on the edge of the cushion. Leaning forward, he balanced his hands between his knees and rotated his hat with his fingers. Luke had sat on this very same sofa a thousand times, but he'd never looked as uncomfortable as he did now.

"I came to apologize for the last time we spoke."

"Oh, Luke," she whispered, sitting in the overstuffed chair across from him, "I felt bad afterward, too. Why do we argue like that? Some days I feel like we're growing further and further apart, and I don't want that."

"I'd like to suggest that we put an end to this nonsense, but you've made your views plain enough."

"You still want to take care of me?"

"I don't think that's so wrong."

"I know." She sighed, tired of repeating the same arguments. "But I'm fully capable of doing that myself."

"Right," he said with deadly softness. "You took care of yourself pretty well during that snowstorm, didn't you?"

"Why don't you throw Eric Wilson in my face while you're at it? I thought you came because you regretted our last argument, but it looks to me like you're eager to start another one."

"All right," he shouted, "I'll stop! You asked me not to bring up the distasteful subject of marriage and

I agreed. It's just that—" He clamped his mouth shut. "We're better off dropping the subject entirely," he finished stiffly.

"I feel terrible when we argue," Kate whispered.

"So do I, Princess."

Although his tone was light, Kate heard the distress in his voice. It filled her with regret and she longed for something comforting to say, something that would ease this awkwardness between them, and return a sense of balance to their relationship.

"Do you need anything, Kate?"

"No. I'm fine," she rushed to assure him. She might occasionally date the wrong men and take foolish risks in snowstorms, but she could manage her own life!

Luke glanced around the room, then slowly nodded as if accepting the truth of her words.

"It was thoughtful of you to stop in . . . I mean, it's good to see you and I really am grateful you wanted to clear the air, too."

"Are you saying you missed me while I was away?"

She had, terribly, but until that moment, Kate hadn't been willing to admit it even to herself. Unconsciously she'd been waiting for Thursday, hoping to hear from Luke—but not really expecting to. For the past few days, she'd worked like a demon to unpack her things and make her apartment presentable. And all along it had been an effort to prove to Luke how efficient and capable she actually was. After falling on her face so many times, she wanted this transition from the ranch house to her first apartment to go off without a hitch. It was a matter of pride.

They were like polite strangers with each other and Kate still couldn't think of any clever remark or probing question to ease this tension between them.

"Have you eaten?" Luke asked brusquely. "I thought I'd take you to dinner. I realize I'm not giving you much notice and I read somewhere that women don't like a man to take things for granted, so if you don't want to go, I'll understand."

He sounded as though he expected her to reject his invitation. "I'd love to have dinner with you," she said, unable to hide a smile.

Luke seemed shocked by her easy acquiescence.

Kate stood up, stretching luxuriously. "If you'll give me a moment, I'll freshen up," she said, unable to keep the happiness out of her voice.

Luke rose then, and his presence seemed to fill every corner of her compact living room. Only a few scant inches separated them. With one finger, he tilted her chin and looked deeply into her eyes. "You honestly missed me?" he whispered.

For some unexplained reason, her throat squeezed shut and Kate was forced to answer him without words. She cradled his face between both hands and gazed up at him, nodding fervently.

Luke's eyes darkened and she thought he meant to kiss her. Just when she was prepared to slip into his arms and raise her mouth to his, he pulled loose from her light grasp and stepped back. Kate was forced to swallow her disappointment.

"I was thinking about that pizza parlor in Riversdale," he said gruffly.

"Pizza sounds wonderful," Kate said.

"Then it's settled."

Kate didn't bother to change clothes, but ran a brush through her hair and refreshed her makeup. A few minutes later, she was ready to leave. Luke stood at the front door, and as she approached him, his appreciative look sent small flutters of awareness through her body.

Companionably they drove the thirty miles to Riversdale. By mutual and unspoken agreement they both avoided any subject that would cause them to disagree.

The restaurant, Pizza Mania, was known throughout the county for its excellent Italian cuisine. The room was dimly lit, and the wooden tables were covered with red-checkered cloths. Since it was a weeknight, the place didn't seem especially busy.

Luke's hand guided her to a table in the middle of the homey room. Service was prompt and they quickly placed their order for a large sausage-and-black-olive pizza. Kate also ordered a raw vegetable platter with yogurt-herb dip, and she laughed at the disdainful expression on Luke's face. A few minutes later, she laughed again.

"What's so funny now?"

"I just remembered the last time I ate pizza from Pizza Mania. It was when Rorie had just arrived—remember?—and she and I were cooking dinner for Clay and Skip. I made a lemon meringue pie and Rorie had spent the entire afternoon cooking up this seafood sauce."

"Where does the pizza come in?"

Kate told Luke about the disastrous dinner, and the smiled slightly, shaking his head. "Rorie must have been devastated."

"Actually she was a pretty good sport about the whole thing. We called Pizza Mania, ordered two large pizzas, and afterward sat in the living room around the piano for a while."

As she thought back to that night all those months ago, Kate realized it was then she'd realized how hard Clay was fighting not to fall in love with Rorie. Kate suspected it when she noticed how he tried not to gaze in Rorie's direction. Then, later in the evening, when he drove Kate home, he said barely a word and gently kissed her cheek after he walked her to the door. A peck on the cheek, the way he'd kiss a younger sister.

"What's wrong?" Luke asked gently.

"Nothing," Kate hurried to say, forcing a smile. "What makes you ask?" She was relieved at the appearance of their vegetable appetizer, immediately reaching for a carrot stick.

"Your eyes looked kind of sad just now."

Kate concentrated on munching her carrot, amazed at the way Luke always seemed to know what she was thinking. But then, sometimes he didn't.... "That night was the first time I realized I was losing Clay to Rorie. My whole world was about to fall in on me and I felt powerless to do anything to stop it. It didn't mean I stopped trying, of course—it hurt too much to accept without putting up a fight." She paused and helped herself to a zucchini strip. "Enough about me. It seems I'm the only one we ever discuss. How was your trip to New Mexico?" she asked brightly, determined to change the subject.

"Good." He didn't elaborate. His gaze held hers, the mood warm and comfortable. "There are going to be a few changes around the Circle L in the coming months. I don't want you to be surprised when you find out I'm adding a couple of outbuildings and doing some remodeling on the house.''

Although he spoke in a conversational tone, Kate wasn't fooled. "The Circle L belongs to you now. I expect there'll be plenty of changes, but don't worry about offending me or Dad.''

He nodded and his dark eyes brightened with his dreams for the future. "I intend to turn it into one of the top cattle ranches on the West Coast within the next fifteen years.''

"I'm sure you'll do it, Luke." And she was.

He seemed pleased by her confidence in him. Kate couldn't help believing in Luke. In the ten years he'd worked for her father, he'd initiated several successful breeding programs. With each passing year, Devin had turned more and more of the ranch business over to Luke. Her father had become only a figurehead. More than once, Kate could remember hearing Devin say that he couldn't understand why Luke would continue working for him when it was obvious the foreman was more than capable of maintaining his own spread. At one time, Kate had thought money was the issue, but that obviously wasn't the case.

"Why'd you delay buying your own ranch for so long?" Kate asked, just as their pizza arrived. Their waitress remained standing at their table and studied them so blatantly that Luke turned to her.

"Is something wrong?" he asked sharply.

"No...not at all. Enjoy your dinner." She backed away from their table and returned to the counter, where two other employees were waiting. Almost immediately the three huddled together and started whispering.

Luke chose to ignore their waitress's strange behavior and lifted a steaming piece, thick with gooey melted cheese and spicy sausage, onto Kate's dinner plate. Then he served himself.

"Now, where were we?" Luke asked.

"I wanted to know why you didn't buy your own ranch long before now."

"You don't want to know the answer to that, Princess."

"Of course I do. I wouldn't have asked you otherwise," she insisted.

"All right," Luke said, settling back in his chair. He looked at her, eyes thoughtful. "I had a minor problem. I was in love with the boss's daughter and she was crazy about me, only she didn't know it. In fact, she'd gotten herself engaged to someone else. I was afraid that if I moved away she'd never realize how I felt—or how she did—and frankly, I didn't think I could ever love anyone the way I do her."

Kate focused her attention on her meal. The knot in her throat was almost choking her. "You're right about...me not loving Clay," she admitted softly. No matter how hard she tried, she couldn't raise her eyes high enough to meet his.

"What did you just say?"

"I... You were right about me and Clay. I could never feel for him the things a wife should feel for her husband. I'd adored him for years, but that love was only an adolescent fantasy."

She was well aware of the seriousness of her admission, and the room seemed to go still with her words. The music from the juke box faded, the clatter from the kitchen dimmed, and the voices from those around them seemed to disappear altogether.

"I didn't ever think I'd hear you admit that," Luke said softly, and his face filled with tenderness.

"I tried to tell you the night after I had dinner with Clay and Rorie, but you were so angry with me... because I was moving." She laughed lightly, hoping to break the unexpected tension that had leapt between them.

"Does this mean you're also admitting you love me?"

"I've never had a problem with that—"

Kate was interrupted by an elderly man who strolled up to their table. With a good deal of ceremony, he lifted a violin to his chin and played a bittersweet love song.

"I didn't know they had strolling violinists here," Kate said when the man had finished. Everyone in the restaurant stopped to applaud.

"This next song is dedicated to the two of you," the man said proudly, "that the love in your hearts will blossom for each other into a bouquet of *May* flowers."

It wasn't until he'd finished the third song that Kate noticed he didn't stroll to any of the other tables. He seemed to be playing only for them. Some of the customers apparently realized this, too, and gathered behind Luke and Kate in order to get a better view of the musician.

"Thank you," Kate said as the last notes faded.

The man lowered his instrument to his side. "You two have become quite a sensation in Nightingale and beyond. We at Pizza Mania are honored that you've chosen our restaurant for a romantic evening. We want to do our part to bring the two of you together in wedded bliss."

"And you're suggesting the month of May?" Kate asked, referring to his comment about a bouquet of flowers.

"It would be an excellent choice," the violinist said, grinning broadly.

"I think it's time we left," Luke said, frowning. He reached for his wallet, but the violinist stopped him. "Please, your pizza's on the house. It's an honor that you chose to dine in our humble establishment."

From the tight set of Luke's mouth, Kate realized he wanted to argue, but more urgent in his mind was the need to escape. He took Kate by the hand and headed for the door.

"Your leftover pizza," their waitress called after them, handing Luke a large white box, as she cast Kate an envious glance.

Luke couldn't seem to get out of the parking lot fast enough. Kate waited until they were on the road before she spoke. "I take it this is the first time that's happened to you?"

Luke laughed shortly. "Not really, only I didn't pick up on it as easily as you. Several people have made odd comments about certain months, but until now, I didn't realize what they were actually saying."

"It's kind of funny when you think about it. Half the county's got money riding on our wedding day, and Fred Garner's making a killing raising and lowering the odds." Suddenly the lottery was the most comical thing Kate had ever heard of, and she started to laugh. She slumped against the side of the cab, holding her sides. She was laughing so hard, her stomach hurt. Tears ran down her cheeks and she wiped them away in an effort to regain control. The wedding lottery and everyone's subtle interference wasn't really so terribly funny, but Luke's disgruntled reaction was. He didn't seem to find any of this the least bit amusing.

"Come on, Luke," she said, still chuckling. "There's a good deal of humor in this situation."

He gave a short snort.

"Don't be such a killjoy. I've been getting free advice from the butcher, Sally Daley, the paperboy and just about everyone else in town. It's only fair that you put up with a few of their comments, too."

"One might think you'd take some of that free advice."

"What?" she cried. "And ruin their fun?"

Luke was oddly quiet for the remainder of the trip into Nightingale. He stopped at her building, walked her to her door with barely another word, then turned and walked away. No good-night kiss, no mention of seeing her again.

This was the last thing she'd expected. For the entire drive home, she'd been thinking about how good it would feel when Luke held her and kissed her. She'd decided to invite him in for coffee, hoping he'd accept. But this was even worse than Clay's peck on the cheek all those months ago.

"Luke..."

He stopped abruptly at the sound of her voice, then turned back. His eyes seemed to burn into hers as he came toward her, and she stumbled into his arms. His mouth, hot and hungry, sought hers in a kiss that scorched her senses.

His fingers plunged deep into her hair, releasing the French braid and plowing through the twisted strands of blond hair.

Instinctively Kate reached up and slid her arms tightly around his shoulders, feeling so much at home in his arms that it frightened her. She trembled with the knowledge, but she didn't have time to analyze her feelings. Not when her world was in chaos. She clung to him as though she were rocketing into a fathomless sky.

Luke broke away from her, his face a study of hope and confusion. "I never know where I stand with you, Kate." With that, he stroked her hair and quickly returned to his truck.

Kate was reeling from the effects of Luke's kiss. If she hadn't leaned against the front door, she might have slumped onto the walkway, so profound was her reaction.

"Luke," she called, shocked by how weak her voice sounded. "Would you like to come inside for coffee? We could talk about . . . things."

Slowly a smile eased its way across his handsome features. "I don't dare, Princess, because the way I feel right now, I might not leave until morning. If then."

Flustered by the truth of his words, Kate unlocked her door and let herself inside.

She gulped a deep breath and stood in the middle of the living room with her hand planted over her rampaging heart. "You're in love with him, Kate Logan," she told herself. "Head over heels in love with a man and fighting him every step of the way."

Groaning, she buried her face in her hands. She didn't understand why she'd been fighting him so hard. She did realize that Luke wouldn't have spent years building up her father's ranch if he hadn't loved her. He could have left anytime, gone anywhere, to buy his own ranch, but he'd stayed at the Circle L. He honestly loved her!

Now that she knew what she wanted, Kate still didn't know what to do about it.

She guessed Luke was planning to court her; if that was the case, one more dinner with him would be enough. They'd be officially engaged by the end of the evening. She'd bet on it!

To her disappointment, Kate didn't hear from Luke the following day. Fridays were generally busy around the ranch, so she decided the next move would have to come from her.

Early Saturday morning she compiled a grocery list, intent on inviting Luke over for a home-cooked meal. She was reviewing her cookbooks, searching for a special dessert recipe, when she was suddenly distracted by the memory of her kiss. Closing her eyes, she relived the way she'd felt that night. She smiled to herself, admitting how eager she was to feel that way again.

If only she'd listened to her heart all these weeks instead of her pride. Happiness bubbled up inside her like the fizz in champagne.

She tried phoning Luke, but there wasn't any answer, so she decided to do the shopping first. She reached for her coat, and walked the few blocks to the Safeway store.

It must had been her imagination, but it seemed that everyone stopped what they were doing and watched her as she pushed her cart down the aisles.

When she'd finished buying her groceries, she headed over to the drugstore and bought a couple of scented candles. Once again, everyone seemed to stop and stare at her.

"Kate," Sally Daley said, walking toward her. The older woman was shaking her head, eyes brimming with sympathy. She reached for Kate's hand and patted it gently. "How are you doing, dear?"

"Fine," Kate said, puzzled.

Sally's mouth dropped. "You don't know then, do you?"

"Know what?"

"Luke Rivers took Betty Hammond to dinner, and the two of them danced all night at the Red Bull. Why, everyone in town's buzzing with it. People are saying he's lost patience with you and is going to marry Betty. Really, dear, every woman in town thinks you'd be crazy to let a man like Luke Rivers get away."

Kate was so shocked she could hardly breathe. "I see," she murmured, pretending it really didn't matter.

"You poor child," Sally said compassionately. "Don't let your pride get in the way."

"I won't," Kate promised, barely able to find her voice.

"I do worry about you, Kate, dear. I have this terrible feeling you're going to end up thirty and all alone."

CHAPTER ELEVEN

THIRTY AND ALL ALONE. The words echoed in Kate's mind as she walked the short distance to her apartment. Tears burned her eyes, but somehow she'd dredged up the courage to smile and assure Sally that Luke was free to date whomever he pleased. In fact, she'd even managed to laugh lightly and say that she hoped Luke's dating Betty would finally put an end to all this wedding-lottery nonsense.

Walking at a clipped pace, she kept her head lowered and headed directly back to her apartment, clutching her purchases to her chest. By the time she let herself in the front door, her face was streaked with tears, although she'd used every ounce of fortitude she possessed to keep them at bay.

No doubt Sally would have the story of her meeting with Kate all over town by evening. Not that it mattered. By now, the residents of Nightingale should be accustomed to hearing gossip about her and Luke.

Luke. The mere thought of him, and her heart constricted painfully. He'd given up on her and now she'd lost him, too. Only it hurt so much more than when Clay had broken their engagement. A hundred times more.

Wiping the tears from her eyes, she struggled to take in all that had happened to her in the past few weeks. It seemed every time she found her balance and secured her footing, something would happen to send her teetering again. Would it never end? Was her life destined to be an endless struggle of one emotional pain following on the heels of another?

She set her bags on the floor, and without bothering to remove her coat, slumped into the overstuffed chair.

"Okay," she said aloud. "Luke took Betty Hammond out to dinner and dancing. It doesn't have to mean anything."

But it did. In her heart Kate was sure Luke planned to do exactly as Sally suggested. He'd made it plain from the first that he wanted a wife, and like a fool, Kate had repeatedly turned him down. He loved her, or so he claimed, and Kate had doubted him. Now she wondered if perhaps he didn't love her enough. But over and over again, Luke had insisted she needed him—and he'd been right.

Closing her eyes, she tried to picture her life without Luke. A chill ran down her spine as an intense wave of loneliness swept over her.

Someone pounded at the door, but before Kate could answer it, Luke strode into the apartment. Having to face him this way, when she was least prepared, put her at a clear disadvantage. Hurriedly she painted on a bright smile.

"Hello, Luke," she said, trying to sound breezy and amused. "What's this I hear about you and Betty?"

"You heard already?" He looked stunned.

"Good heavens, yes. You don't honestly expect something like that to stay quiet, do you?"

"When . . . who told you?"

"I went to the grocery store and ran into Sally Daley."

"That explains it," he said, pacing her carpet with abrupt, impatient steps. He stopped suddenly and turned to study her. "It doesn't bother you that I'm seeing Betty?"

"Good grief, no," she lied. "Should it? Would you like some coffee?"

"No."

Desperate for a chance to escape and compose herself, Kate almost ran into the kitchen and poured herself a cup, keeping her back to him all the while.

"You seem to be downright happy about this," he accused, following her into the small, windowless room.

"Of course I'm pleased. I think it's wonderful when two people fall in love, don't you?"

"I'm not in love with Betty," he said angrily.

"Actually I think dating Betty is a wonderful way to kill all the rumors that are floating around about us," she said, finally turning to face him. She held her coffee cup close, though, for protection.

Rubbing his neck, Luke continued his pacing in the kitchen. "I thought you might be . . . jealous."

"Me?" She couldn't very well admit she'd been dying inside from the moment Sally had told her. Her pride wouldn't allow that. "Now why would I feel like that?"

"I don't know," Luke barked. "Why would you?"

Before Kate could answer, he stormed out of the apartment, leaving her so frustrated she wanted to weep.

"You could have told him how you feel," she reprimanded herself aloud. "Why are you such a fool when it comes to Luke Rivers? Why? Why? Why?"

"I SAW LUKE YESTERDAY," Rorie said, watching Kate closely as they sat across from each other in a booth at Nellie's.

"That's nice," she said, pretending indifference and doing a grand job at it.

"He was with Betty Hammond."

Kate's breath caught in her throat at the unexpected rush of pain. "I . . . see."

"Do you?" Rorie inquired softly. "I swear I could shake the pair of you. I don't know when I've ever met two more stubborn people in my life. You look like one of the walking wounded, and Luke's got a chip on his shoulder the size of a California redwood."

"I'm sure you're mistaken." Kate concentrated on stirring her coffee, and she avoided Rorie's eyes. Her heart felt like a ball of lead.

"When was the last time you two talked?"

"A couple of days ago."

"Honestly, Kate, I can't understand what's wrong with you. Clay and I thought . . . we hoped everything would fall into place after you moved to the apartment. Now it seems exactly the opposite has happened."

"Luke's free to date whomever he pleases, just the way I am."

"There's only one person you want and that's Luke Rivers and we both know it," Rorie said with an exasperated sigh. "I shouldn't have said that. It's just that I hate the thought of you two being so miserable when you're both so much in love with each other."

"Is love always this painful?" Kate asked, her question barely audible.

Rorie shrugged. "It was with Clay and me, and sometimes I feel it must be for everyone sooner or later. Think about it, Kate. If you honestly love Luke, why are you fighting the very thing you want most?''

"I don't know," she admitted reluctantly.

They parted a few minutes later. Kate felt a new sense of certainty and resolve. She *did* love Luke and if she didn't do something soon, she was going to lose him.

She drove to the Circle L, her heart in her throat the entire way. Luke's truck was parked behind the house, and she left her car beside it, hurrying through the cold to the back door. Luke didn't respond to her knock, which didn't surprise her, since it was unusual for him to be in at this time of day. But she couldn't find him outside, either, and even Bill didn't know where he was.

Making a rapid decision, she let herself into the house and started preparations for the evening meal. It gave her a way of passing the time. Dinner was in the oven and she was busy making a fresh green salad, when the back door opened and Luke walked into the kitchen.

Apparently he hadn't noticed her car because he stopped dead, shock written in every feature, when he saw her standing at the sink.

Kate held her breath for a moment, then dried her hands on the dish towel she'd tucked into her waistband. She struggled to give the impression that she was completely at ease, tried to act as though she made dinner for him every evening.

"Hello, Luke," she said to break the silence that had been growing heavier by the second.

He blinked. "I suppose you're looking for an explanation."

Kate wasn't sure she knew what he meant.

"Taking Betty out Friday night was a mistake."

"Then why'd you do it?"

"So you'd be jealous. The night you and I went out, I was furious at the way you started laughing, and talking as though you never planned to marry me. I wanted you to know you weren't the only fish in the sea. Only my idea backfired."

"It did?" Not so far as Kate was concerned—she'd been pretty darn worried.

"That wasn't all that went wrong. Betty saw I was in town on Saturday and started following me," he explained. "I swear I had no intention of seeing her again, but before I knew what was happening, her arm was linked with mine and we were strolling through the middle of town together."

"Betty's a nice girl."

He frowned. "Yes, I suppose she is. I'd forgotten it doesn't bother you who I date, does it? You've never been one to give in to fits of jealousy."

"I was so jealous I wanted to die."

"You were? You could have fooled me."

"Believe me, I tried to," Kate murmured.

"Exactly what are you doing here?"

"I fixed dinner," Kate said sheepishly. She'd admitted how she felt about Luke seeing Betty and she'd be an idiot to stop there. "I've got pork chops in the oven, along with scalloped potatoes and an acorn squash," she rattled off without pausing for breath, then gathering her resolve, casually added, "and if you're still asking, I'll marry you."

That stopped Luke cold. When he finally spoke he sounded strangely calm. "What did you just say?"

"There's pork chops and potatoes and—"

"Not that. The part about marrying me."

She struggled to hold on to what remained of her tattered pride. "If you're still asking me to marry you, then I'd be honored to be your wife."

"I'm still asking."

Kate dropped her gaze and her throat squeezed tight. "You've been right about so many things lately. I do need you. I guess I was waiting all this time for you to admit you needed *me*, only you never did."

Luke rubbed a hand over his face. "Not need you?" he asked, his voice filled with shock and wonder. "I think my life would be an empty shell without you, Kate. I couldn't bear the thought of living one day to the next if you weren't at my side to share everything with me—all the good things that are in store for us. I've waited so long, Kate."

"You honestly do love me, don't you?" she whispered.

For a long, long moment Luke said nothing. "I tried not to. For years I stood by helpless and frustrated, watching you break out in hives with excitement every time Clay Franklin came close. I realized then it was a schoolgirl crush, but you never seemed to get over him. Instead of improving, things got worse. How could I let you know how I felt?"

"Couldn't you have said something? Anything?"

A flicker of pain crossed his face. "No. You were so infatuated with Clay I didn't dare. It wouldn't have done any good—although only God knows how you managed not to figure it out yourself. The first time Rorie met me, she guessed."

"Rorie knew all along?"

Luke shook his head in bewildered amusement. "We were a lovesick pair a few months back—Rorie in love with Clay and me crazy about you. All this time, I thought I'd kept my feelings secret, and then I discovered everyone in town knew.''

"Betty Hammond didn't,'' Kate countered.

"No, but she should have. I've never wanted anyone but you, Kate Logan. I haven't for years. Somehow I always kept hoping you'd see the light.''

"Oh, Luke.'' She took a step toward him, her eyes full of emotion. "Are you going to stand way over there on the other side of the room? I need you so much.''

For every step Kate took, Luke managed three. When they reached each other, she put her arms around his waist, hugging him tight. She felt the surge of his heart and closed her eyes, succumbing to the wave of love that threatened to overwhelm her.

Luke's hand was gentle on her hair. "Do you love me, Kate?''

She discovered she couldn't speak, so she wildly nodded her head. Her hands framed his face and she spread light, eager kisses over his mouth and nose and eyes, letting her lips explain what was in her heart.

"I love you,'' he whispered. "If you marry me, I promise I'll do everything I can to make you happy.'' His eyes shone with delight and a kind of humility that touched Kate's very soul. Gone was the remoteness he'd displayed so often these past few weeks.

"Oh, Luke, I can hardly wait to be your wife,'' she said. "Didn't you once say something about a December wedding?''

"Kate, that's only a few weeks from now.''

"Yes, I know. But Christmas is such a lovely time of year for a wedding. We'll decorate the church in holly, and all the bridesmaids will have long red dresses. . . .''

"Kate, dear Lord, you mean it, don't you?" His voice was low and husky.

"I've never meant anything more in my life. I love you. We're going to have such a good life together, Luke Rivers."

He kissed her then, with a hunger that spoke of his years of longing. Dragging his mouth from hers, he buried it in the gentle curve of her neck.

"I want children, Kate. I want to fill this home with so much love that the walls threaten to burst with it."

For a breathless moment, they did nothing more than gaze at each other as they shared the dream.

Kate smiled up at him, and as her hands mapped his face, loving each strong feature, she was amazed at how easily this happiness had come to her once she let go of her pride.

Luke's mouth settled on hers, his kiss gentle, almost reverent, as though he couldn't yet believe she was in his home and eager to be his wife.

As Kate wrapped her arms around his neck, her gaze fell on the calendar. December was a good month, and she seemed to remember that Pastor Wilkins had placed a sizable wager on the fifteenth. That sounded good to Kate.

Very good indeed.

EPILOGUE

THE SUN SHONE clear and bright in the late July afternoon, two years after Rorie Campbell's car had broken down near Nightingale. Kate was making a fresh pitcher of iced tea when Rorie knocked on the back door.

"Let yourself in," Kate called. "The screen door's unlocked."

A moment later Rorie entered the kitchen, looking slightly frazzled. "How did your afternoon at the library go?" Kate asked, as she added ice cubes to the tall pitcher.

"Very well, thanks."

"Katherine's still sleeping," Kate told her.

Rorie's eyes softened as she gazed out at the newly constructed patio where her baby slept under the shade of the huge oak tree.

"It was such a lovely afternoon I kept her outside." Kate wiped her hands dry. She poured them each a tall glass of iced tea, and carried a tray of tea and cookies onto the patio.

The nine-month old infant stirred when Rorie stood over the portable crib and protectively placed her hand on the sleeping baby's back. When she turned, her eyes fell on Kate's protruding abdomen. "How are *you* feeling?"

"Like a blimp." Kate's hands rested on her swollen stomach and she patted it gently. "The doctor told me it would probably be another two weeks."

"Two weeks!" Rorie said, looking sympathetic.

"I know, and I was hoping Junior would choose to arrive this week. I swear to you, Rorie, when you were pregnant with Katherine you positively glowed. You made everything look so easy, so natural."

Rorie laughed. "I did?"

"I feel miserable. My legs are swollen, my hands and feet look like they've been inflated. I swear, there isn't a single part of my body that's normal-sized anymore."

Rorie laughed. "The last few weeks are always like that. I think the main difference is that Katherine was born in October, when the weather was much cooler."

With some difficulty Kate crossed her legs. "I only hope our baby will be as good-natured as Katherine. She barely fussed the whole time she was here."

"Her Uncle Skip thinks she's going to start walking soon."

"I think he's right." Pressing a hand to her ribs, Kate shifted her position. She was finding it difficult to sit comfortably for longer than a few minutes at a time.

"Oh—" Rorie set her iced tea aside "—I almost forgot." She hurried back into the kitchen and returned a moment later with a hardbound children's book. "I received my first copies of *Nightsong's Adventures* in the mail yesterday. Kate, I can't even begin to tell you how thrilled I was when I held this book in my hands."

Kate reverently laid the book in her lap and slowly turned the pages. "The illustrations are fantastic—almost as good as the story!"

"The reviews have been excellent. One critic said he expected it to become a children's classic, which I know is probably ridiculous, but I couldn't help feeling excited about it."

"It isn't ridiculous, and I'm sure your publisher knows that, otherwise they wouldn't have been so eager to buy your second book."

"You know, the second sale was every bit as exciting as the first," Rorie admitted with a soft smile.

"Just think, within a few years our children will be reading your stories and attending school together. They're bound to be the best of friends."

"It's enough to boggle the mind, isn't it?"

Before Rorie could respond, the baby woke and they watched, delighted, as she sat up in the portable crib. When she saw her mother sitting next to Kate, she grinned, her dark eyes twinkling. She raised her chubby arms, reaching for Rorie.

Rorie stood and lifted Katherine out of the crib, kissing the little girl's pudgy cheeks. "I'd better get back home. Thanks so much for watching Katherine for me. I promised I'd pinch-hit for the new librarian if she ever needed me, and I didn't think I could refuse her even if it was at the last minute like this."

"It wasn't any problem, so don't worry. And tell Mary she should visit her sister more often so I get the opportunity to watch Katherine every once in a while."

"Call me later and let me know how you're feeling."

Kate nodded, promising that she would.

Ten minutes after Rorie and Katherine left, Luke drove up and parked in the back of the house. Standing on the porch, Kate waved to her husband.

Luke joined her, placing an arm around what once had been a trim waist, and led the way into the kitchen. "You okay?" His gaze was tender and warm.

Kate wasn't exactly sure how to answer that. She was miserable. Excited. Frightened. Eager. So many emotions were coming at her, she didn't know which one to respond to first.

"Kate?"

"I feel fine." There was no need to list her complaints, but all of a sudden she felt *funny*. She didn't know of any other way to describe it. As Rorie had explained, there were a dozen different aches and pains the last few weeks of any pregnancy. Given time, Kate figured she'd grow accustomed to this feeling, too.

Luke kissed her then, his mouth gentle over hers. "Did you have a busy day with Katherine?"

"She slept almost the entire time, but I think Rorie knew she would." Leaning forward, Kate kissed her husband's jaw. "I made some iced tea. Want some?"

"Please."

When Kate reached inside the cupboard for a glass, a sharp pain split her side. She let out a soft cry.

"Kate?"

Clenching her swollen abdomen, Kate's startled gaze flew to Luke. "Oh, my goodness. I just felt a pain."

Luke paled. "You're in labor?"

Smiling, wide-eyed, she nodded slowly. "I must be. I didn't expect them to start off so strong."

Luke was across the kitchen beside her. "Now what?"

"I think I should call the doctor."

"No." Luke's arm flew out as if holding out his hand would halt the course of nature. "I'll call. Stay there. Don't move."

"But, Luke—"

"For heaven's sake, Kate, don't argue with me now. We're about to have a baby!"

He said this as if it were a recent discovery. She noted as he reached for the phone that he'd gone deathly pale. When he finished talking to the doctor, he gave her a panicked look, then announced that Doc Adams wanted them to go straight to the hospital. As soon as the words left his mouth, he shot to the bedroom and returned a moment later with her packed suitcase. He halted abruptly when he saw she was on the phone.

"Who are you calling?"

"Dad and Dorothea. I promised I would."

"Dear Lord, Kate, would you kindly let me do the telephoning?"

"All right." She gave him the receiver and started toward the bedroom to collect the rest of her things. If he thought that talking on the phone was too taxing for her, fine. She'd let him do it. The years had taught her that arguing with Luke was fruitless.

"Kate," he yelled. "Don't wander off."

"Luke, I just want to gather my things before we leave." A pain started to work its way around her back and she paused, flattening her hands across her abdomen. Slowly she raised her head and smiled up at her husband. "Oh, Luke, the baby..."

Luke dropped the telephone and rushed to her side. "Now?"

"No." She laughed gently and touched his loving face. "It'll be hours yet. Oh! I just felt another pain—a bad one."

He swallowed hard and gripped both her hands in his own. "I've been waiting for this moment for nine months and I swear to you, Kate, I've never been more frightened in my life."

"Don't look so worried." Her hands caressed his face and she kissed him gently, offering him what reassurance she could.

He exhaled noisily, then gave her a brisk little nod. Without warning, he lifted her into his arms, ignoring her protests, and carried her out the door to the truck. Once he'd settled her in the seat, he returned to the house for her bag.

"Luke," she called after him, "I really would like to talk to Dad and Dorothea."

"I'll phone them from the hospital. No more arguing, Kate. I'm in charge here."

Only another sharp pain—and her regard for Luke's feelings—kept her from breaking out in laughter.

TEN LONG HOURS LATER, Kate lay in the hospital bed, eyes closed in exhaustion. When she opened them, she discovered her father standing over her. Dorothea was next to him, looking as pleased and proud as Kate's father. Devin took his daughter's hand in his own and squeezed it gently. "How do you feel, little mother?"

"Wonderful. Did they let you see him? Oh, Dad, he's so beautiful!"

Her father nodded, looking as though he were unable to speak for a moment. "Luke's with Matthew now. He looks so big sitting in that rocking chair, holding his son.''

''I don't think I've ever seen Luke wear an expression quite like that before,'' Dorothea murmured. ''So tender and loving.''

Devin concurred with a hard nod of his head. ''When Luke came into the waiting room to tell us Matthew Devin had been born, there were tears in his eyes. I'll tell you, Kate, that man loves you.''

''I know, Dad, and I love him, too.''

Devin patted her hand. ''You go ahead and rest, Princess. Dorothea and I'll be back tomorrow.''

When Kate opened her eyes a second time, Luke was there. She held out her hand to him and smiled dreamily. ''I couldn't have done it without you. Thank you for staying with me.''

''Staying with you,'' he echoed softly, his fingers brushing the tousled curls from her face. ''Nothing on this earth could have kept me away. I swear, Kate, I would have done anything to spare you that pain. Anything.'' His voice was raw with the memory of those last hours.

Her smile was one of comfort. ''It only lasted a little while and we have a beautiful son to show for it.''

''All these months when we've talked about the baby,'' he said, his eyes glazed, ''he seemed so unreal to me, and then you were in the delivery room and in so much agony. I felt so helpless. I wanted so much to be able to help you and there was nothing I could do. Then Matthew was born and, Kate, I looked at him and I swear something happened to my heart. The overwhelming surge of love I felt for that baby, that tiny person, was so strong, so powerful, I could barely breathe. I thought I was going to break down and start weeping right there in front of everyone.''

"Oh, Luke.''

"There's no way I could ever thank you for all you've given me, Kate Rivers.''

"Yes, there is,'' she said with a smile. "Just love me.''

"I do,'' he whispered, his voice husky with emotion. "I always will.''

Have You Ever Wondered If You Could Write A Harlequin Novel?

Here's great news—Harlequin is offering a series of cassette tapes to help you do just that. Written by Harlequin editors, these tapes give practical advice on how to make your characters—and your story—come alive. There's a tape for each contemporary romance series Harlequin publishes.

Mail order only

All sales final

THE LOVES OF A CENTURY...

Join American Romance in a nostalgic look back at the Twentieth Century—at the lives and loves of American men and women from the turn-of-the-century to the dawn of the year 2000.

Journey through the decades from the dance halls of the 1900s to the discos of the seventies ... from Glenn Miller to the Beatles ... from Valentino to Newman ... from corset to miniskirt ... from beau to Significant Other.

Relive the moments ... recapture the memories.

Look now for the CENTURY OF AMERICAN ROMANCE series in Harlequin American Romance. In one of the four American Romance titles appearing each month, for the next twelve months, we'll take you back to a decade of the Twentieth Century, where you'll relive the years and rekindle the romance of days gone by.

Don't miss a day of the CENTURY OF AMERICAN ROMANCE.

The women...the men...the passions...
the memories....

CAR-1